"Effortlessly readable, with a heroine whose gentle but determined nature makes her easy to root for. . . . A sweet, satisfying story about finding your place."—*Booklist*

"A good bet for an intergenerational book club."—*Kirkus Reviews*

"Blecher has created a sweet and realistically vulnerable character who longs to feel validated and respected."—*Publishers Weekly*

"A beautiful story about learning to speak up and taking risks."
—*School Library Journal*

"A tenderhearted debut that navigates the emotional waters of wanting to stay young and grow up, all at the same time."
—Jodi Kendall, critically acclaimed author of
The Unlikely Story of a Pig in the City

"*Out of Place* is sensitively observed and deeply felt, yet also light on its feet. Some of its components seem, at first, peculiarly shaped, but this I promise you: They are all part of Jennifer Blecher's grand design. By the end, all the loose pieces come together beautifully, seamlessly, surprisingly, as if threaded with magic."
—Jack Cheng, author of the acclaimed *See You in the Cosmos*

"Cove may feel out of place, but she'll quickly find her place in readers' hearts. Her voice glows like a Menemsha sunset in Jennifer Blecher's moving debut."—Julie Berry, author of
The Scandalous Sisterhood of Prickwillow Place

This book is a work of fiction. References to real people, events, establishments, organizations, or locales are intended only to provide a sense of authenticity, and are used to advance the fictional narrative. All other characters, and all incidents and dialogue, are drawn from the author's imagination and are not to be construed as real.

Library of Congress Cataloging-in-Publication Data
Names: Blecher, Jennifer, author.
Title: Out of place / written by Jennifer Blecher.
Description: New York, NY : Greenwillow Books, an imprint of HarperCollins
    publishers, [2019] | Summary: Twelve-year-old Cove Bernstein yearns for her best friend, Nina,
    who moved to New York City, but with unlikely new friends, Cove discovers that life on Martha's
    Vineyard can be pretty good.
Identifiers: LCCN 2018035033 | ISBN 9780062748607 (paperback)
Subjects: | CYAC: Best friends—Fiction. | Friendship—Fiction. | Creative
    ability—Fiction. | Single-parent families—Fiction. | Moving, Household—Fiction.
Classification: LCC PZ7.B61658 Out 2019 | DDC [Fic]—dc23 LC record available
    at https://lccn.loc.gov/2018035033

20 21 22 23 24 PC/BRR 10 9 8 7 6 5 4 3 2 1

First paperback edition, 2020
Greenwillow Books

JENNIFER BLECHER

Out of Place

Greenwillow Books

AN IMPRINT OF HARPERCOLLINS PUBLISHERS

To Ella, Olivia, and Aven

41.342807, -70.743469. That's where I live in numbers.

Every place on this earth has an address in numbers. It's so people who don't speak the same language can tell each other where they live. So they can find each other anywhere in the world. But that doesn't make any sense, because how would they even ask the question in the first place? How could someone who speaks Chinese ask someone who speaks French where they live and expect an answer?

"Just drop it please, Cove," says Mom when I try and explain how the whole idea is flawed. That's my name. Cove. Cove Bernstein.

"No, it's cool," says her boyfriend. His name is Sean, and he's the reason we're even having this conversation. Because if Sean's allowed to come to breakfast without a shirt on, then I'm allowed to ask why he has long numbers tattooed up and down his arm. Sean tells me that the numbers represent all the important places he's been in his life.

He goes down his arm saying the names. Bali. India. Thailand. Hawaii.

Sean has been a lot of places.

I have only been here. On this island. Martha's Vineyard.

Sean does not have the numbers for Martha's Vineyard on his arm. I think that's one reason why Mom slams her bowl into the sink and says, "Can we please stop talking about numbers."

But I have one more question.

"Why didn't you just use the real names? That way people would know where you've been."

Sean shrugs his bare shoulders and leans back in his chair so that he's balancing on the two rear legs. It's weird to see him sitting in our kitchen chairs, the way his large body covers the entire wood frame so he looks like a genie floating on air. I'm used to seeing Mom sitting in those chairs, or my best friend, Nina. They both like to crisscross their legs on the seat, only Mom sits up very straight and rests her hands in her lap. Nina kind of slumps over and twists her long hair.

But both Mom and Nina take up the right amount of space on the chair. Not like Sean. Although Sean does answer my question, which is not something Mom always does. "I just like keeping some things to myself," he says. "If people know where you've been, they start thinking they can predict where you'll go next."

Last night I heard Mom yelling at Sean. She called him stupid and naive and irresponsible. But this morning at breakfast, I decide that Sean's actually pretty smart. He knows about patterns. How things can fit together and become something new, something totally different from what they used to be when they were all alone. When they were just individual pieces.

I think Sean would understand why I did what I did.

I think he would get it.

For a second I almost tell him.

But I can't tell anyone.

Not yet.

Three Months Earlier

July

"I am the sky," says Mom as we wait behind a line of cars trying to pull into the Artists Market dirt parking lot. "I am the sky and this traffic is the rain. Remember that, Cove. You are the sky. Whatever is happening is just the weather. It will pass."

"I know," I say. Mom is always saying things like that. Whenever something bad happens, she pretends like it's not actually happening. The bad thing is just a passing rainstorm or a star shooting through the night sky. Sometimes I try to think the way she does, but it never works.

When something bad happens, it gets stuck inside me. Like when we got our yearbooks at the end of school and I found out that Hunter Gilford put bunny ears over my head in the class picture. I try to imagine that Hunter's grinning face is being taken away on the back of a stinking garbage truck and dumped into the island trash heap underneath a pile of rotting vegetables. But then I remember that every single person at my school has a copy of the picture, that Sophie and Amelia even circled the bunny ears in black Sharpie because they thought it was so funny, and his face comes right back. Hunter's happy grin lands in my brain, and there's nothing I can do to make it leave.

I look out our truck window. It's hot and dry today, which means that the Artists Market where Mom sells her inspirational quotes is going to be crowded with people stopping by on their way to the beach. They'll be wearing big sunglasses and carrying plastic cups of iced coffee that will leave wet circles on Mom's table.

Mom will smile and act like those wet circles are no big deal, like they're just raindrops falling from the sky. But she'll wipe them up as soon as the people walk away. Maybe that's what Mom should really be saying about bad things. That you have to wipe them away or else they leave marks.

We finally get through the traffic, and Mom drives our truck onto the grass so that we can unload. It's one of my favorite parts of the day, getting to pull our truck into the special area that's reserved for outdoor artists. The ground is bumpy underneath our tires, and I unbuckle my seat belt since we're not on a real road. Sometimes, if we hit a bump at just the right speed, my entire body lifts off the seat and I feel like I'm floating. I feel it deep in my stomach, like maybe I'll keep going up, up, up.

I always come back down, of course. Gravity and all that. But for one second it feels like I won't. Like I'll get to stay floating forever.

The other outdoor artists wave as we pass. Linda, who paints enormous oil paintings of the ocean. Charleston, who makes animal sculptures out of silverware, like birds with fork prongs for wings and pigs with spoons for bellies. Joyce, who sells wool hats even though it's summer and just looking at the thick hats makes me feel hot and itchy.

Mom's table is at the end of a row. I get my folding chair out of the back of the truck and put it next to her table as she arranges her quotes. Mom doesn't sit down because she likes to maintain an aura of welcomeness so people feel comfortable coming up to her table to browse. But she lets me bring a chair. Otherwise I end up leaning my elbows on the table and that messes up the aura.

Aura is very important to Mom, especially when she's selling her quotes. The quotes are words that she writes in fancy cursive with a thick pen that has bristles on the end like a paintbrush. When they're dry, she puts the quotes in painted frames. Sometimes the words Mom writes make people cry. That is a good thing, even though it sounds bad. The crying person will give Mom a long hug and buy the quote. But most people just pick the quotes up and squint their eyes a little, like they're having trouble reading the words. They'll check the back of the frame before putting the quote down on the table. I don't know why they look at the back. There's nothing there. But they always do.

My official job is to help when Mom gets busy. I'm supposed to go back to our truck to get more quotes or count out change. But it's hardly ever busy. So that gives me time to listen.

I love summer. Everything's so easy. This is the life.

The sun feels divine. Simply divine.

Which beach should we go to this afternoon? Norton Point? Long Point? Squibnocket?

Can I please get an icy? Please? Pleeaase?

I hear that last one a lot. That's because Mom's

table is right next to Delphina the icy lady's table. Even though it's technically an artists market, Delphina's allowed to sell her icies because everyone on the island loves Delphina. She's round, just like the huge yellow tub that she scoops her raspberry lemonade icies from, and she has long curly hair that she wraps in colorful string.

When I was younger, some of the summer girls would smile at me while they waited in line to get an icy. They'd say, "Ah, you're so cute. What's your name?" Sometimes they would pat my head, like I was a cat. I know that sounds kind of mean, but it wasn't. It always made me smile. No one does that to me anymore. I guess that's what happens when you get older. Or when you're me. But the good part is, when people don't notice me, I notice them more and more.

The summer girls wear thin rubber flip-flops. Their toenails are painted pink and turquoise and dark blue. They wear T-shirts with words in sparkly letters. *Girl*

Power. Dance Diva. Too Cool for School. They carry their phones in cases that have ears like a bunny. Or a panda bear. Today one is a Hello Kitty.

I notice all the things I don't have.

But I do have Nina. And she doesn't have any of those things, either. But that's not why we're best friends. We're best friends because when we see each other, everything else fades away. Like now, Nina walks out of Grange Hall on the other side of the Artists Market and waves at me. She spins around a post on the covered front porch and I know just what to do. I tell Mom I'll be right back and run through the crowds to the spinning wheel at the playground. Nina meets me there. We each grab a handle and push as hard as we can. Then we jump on, lay on our backs, and look up at the sky. The trees blur together and the clouds blur together and our bodies blur together and we spin into the same person.

But as we spin, Nina doesn't say anything. Not

even when I tell her about the Hello Kitty phone case. I sit up because the wheel has slowed. I'm dizzy from looking up at the clouds, so at first I don't notice. I don't notice that she's crying.

"Do you know?" she asks.

Because that's another thing that happens when we spin—our thoughts combine so we can tell what the other person is thinking.

So I should know why she's crying. I always have before. But I don't.

That's the first terrible thing that happens. The second terrible thing is she tells me.

"We're moving."

"What?"

"We're moving away. Off island. To New York City."

"You can't."

"I know," says Nina. "But we are. My dads just told me this morning. It's the stupid paintings. Some important art guy saw them and he wants to hang them in his gallery in New York City. Dad thinks it's a once-in-a-lifetime opportunity for Papa and that we have to be there to make the most of it. That's how they talk all of a sudden. Like moving to New York City is the most exciting thing ever and if we don't go, the entire world will explode."

Nina's papa, Toby, is a painter. He used to paint lots of things, like the Edgartown Lighthouse and the Aquinnah Cliffs. The Flying Horses Carousel in Oak Bluffs and the fishing huts in Menemsha. Normal island things, like a lot of the other painters at the Artists Market. Then Toby started to paint Nina. Not her actual self, but a combination of shapes that Toby pieces together. The shapes are different colors and textures, but somehow they combine to make Nina. Her long blond hair and pointy chin. Her wide blue eyes. That's when Toby had to move to a bigger corner stall inside Grange Hall because people wanted to stop and talk to him. They started buying Ninas. Lots of them. And Nina's dad, Clark, stopped working on sailboat engines at the marina and became the one who picked us up at school because Toby was busy painting.

"You're going to be famous," I say.

"But I'm going to be gone," says Nina. "I don't want to be gone. Will you spin me?"

I nod. I need to move. I grab a hard metal handle and run as fast as I can. Because I can't look at Nina's face. Her soon-to-be-famous face.

1

After the Artists Market closes, I go to Nina's house. I need to stay close to her, like if I let her out of my sight she'll disappear. We are lying on the floor of her bedroom surrounded by clothes. We're supposed to be making piles. One for clothes to take to New York City, another for clothes that don't fit anymore. Instead, we are looking at the book, even though we've already read it one million times. Even though we know what all the pages say.

The book appeared on Nina's bed at the beginning of the summer. Nina's dads didn't say anything about it, we just found it on her pink-and-white quilt with a Post-it note stuck to the cover that said: *Let us know if you have any questions!* There was a heart at the bottom so we knew Clark had written the note. It was a very bad heart. Toby's heart would have been much better.

There are lots of funny parts of the book. There are drawings of a girl with enormous eyes blowing brown clouds out of her mouth because she's forgotten to brush her teeth and a girl balancing wobbly books on her head because she's trying to walk with good posture. But those aren't the parts we care about. We care about the other parts. The changing body parts. There's one page in particular that Nina is obsessed with. It's the page with the bras.

"I would choose this one," says Nina, pointing to a drawing of a light-blue bra with green polka dots. The bra looks like two triangles held together in the front by a tiny bow. There are other bra choices. A pink one in the shape of a tank top, only without the stomach part. A green one with ruffled trim around the edges. A white one with pink straps that cross in the back. But Nina always chooses the light-blue polka-dot bra.

"I think that one would look good on you," I say.

"You really think so? Can you check me?"

I turn to the page that comes before the bras. Along the bottom are five drawings of a girl standing in front of a bathroom mirror. She's not wearing a shirt, which is weird, but the whole point of the drawings is to see how her body changes. In the first drawing, she has no boobs at all and her hair is wrapped up in a towel. But by the last drawing, she's got huge boobs and her hair has grown long and flowing. The words under the drawings say that it takes five years to grow from drawing one to drawing five. But the words don't say when the growing starts. That's the thing about the book. It thinks it explains everything, but it leaves out all the important parts.

Nina pulls her shirt tight and turns sideways so I

can look. "What do you think?" she asks.

Her shirt is perfectly flat the whole way down her chest. "I think you're still at one."

"Are you sure? Can I see the chart again?" Nina likes charts and numbers. She likes the way things fit together—old boat engine parts that Clark brings home, school math challenges that only work when every step is correct, one-thousand-piece puzzles that she seals with glue and stacks under her bed.

"What about me?" I ask.

I turn sideways and pull my shirt down tight. I'm nervous, because I really want her to say I'm at one, too. Her eyes move from my shoulders, to my belly button, and back up again. I can almost feel my chest tingling, like it's threatening to burst through at that very moment.

"One," she says. "Definitely one."

I'm so relieved that I start to laugh. Then Nina starts to laugh. I don't know why we're laughing, it's just what happens when we're together. Soon we'll put the book back in her pile of old stuffed animals, where we keep it tucked in between Rainbow Dash and Twilight Sparkle. We'll put on our bathing suits and run across the spiky crabgrass in her backyard to Eel Pond. We'll jump into the cool water, feeling the tiny air bubbles tickle the inside of our noses, and our hair spread out weightless around us. We'll be mermaids, do handstand contests on the sandy bottom, or just float on our backs.

Except Nina stops laughing.

"But what do you think I should do now, when it happens?" she asks.

"I don't know," I say. "What do you think I should do?"

When we were laughing, I could forget. Now, I remember. The sounds coming from downstairs aren't just Clark and Toby moving furniture; they're the sounds of them packing boxes. Nina's leaving and everything is ruined.

Because there's something else about those bras in

the book. They aren't just floating in the air. The bras are on fancy padded hangers with dangling price tags. The girls trying them on are standing in dressing rooms with thick purple curtains hanging from golden rods. In one dressing room, a mom is hooking the white bra with the crossing pink straps behind her daughter's back. In a second dressing room, a girl is holding the green bra with the ruffle trim while her mom is holding the pink tank top one. And Nina's light-blue polka-dot bra? That bra is in a third dressing room where a mom is adjusting the strap on her daughter's shoulder.

The thing is, the book doesn't say what to do if you live on an island where there's no bra store with thick purple curtains. Or if you don't have a mom. If you have two dads instead. Or if you have a mom like mine.

But that didn't matter because Nina and I figured out a solution on our own. We would go bra shopping together. When the time came, we were going to ask Nina's dads to take us off island to Target. We were going to tell them that we needed to get something important from the book, so they'd probably know what it was but not ask too many questions. Target is where Molly's mom took Molly to buy bras. Molly said there's a Starbucks in the front of the store. That's where I picture Nina's dads waiting, drinking coffee, while Nina and I go to the back section, just like Molly described.

Molly said Target has so many racks of bras that the straps get tangled together like fishing wire. She said when you pull one bra out to see what it looks like, ten more bras come trailing along with it. And once you find a shape you like, you still have to choose the color. Molly's mom only let her pick between tan and white. But since Nina and I were going together, we would choose way better colors than that.

There'd be no one there to stop us.

It would be just the two of us, like always. And we'd figure it out together.

Or we would have. If Nina wasn't leaving.

3

An hour later I am sitting on the wood dock that leads from Nina's backyard into Eel Pond. My feet are dangling in the clear water. Tiny minnows swirl around my toes. The name Eel Pond sounds icky, like something might swim up and wrap its slimy body around my feet at any minute. But Eel Pond is nothing like that. It's one of my favorite places on the entire island.

Clang. Clang. Clang. The old bell that stands on a wooden pole next to Nina's house rings out. Three rings means dinner's ready. Usually the bell sounds happy, like it's bouncing off its iron shell, excited to do its one job of the day. But tonight it sounds sad. Like it's trapped. Like the bell knows it's being left behind.

"Dinner!" I yell to Nina. Except she can't hear me because she's underwater. When her head pops up above the surface, I try again. This time she hears.

"Let's do one more round," she says, wiping the water from her eyes. "Just a quick one."

"Okay," I say. My stomach is rumbling, but I hate the thought of going inside. "You go first. I'll follow."

We are playing mermaid sisters, which is like regular swimming except with special chin-tucked dives and joined-leg kicks. My favorite part is going under the water and feeling it flow over the top of my head and down my body. Because when I do that, I don't think about anything except arching my back and coming up for air.

Nina dives in front of me, her pointed toes making tiny splashes as she kicks herself down. Usually we only go to where the water lines up with the edge of her backyard. About nine dives. But Nina gets to nine and keeps going. I don't know if she realizes how far she's gone. I don't call out for her to stop. All I think about is staying close. Diving down, arching up. The water flowing through my hair and over my body.

When Nina finally pauses, we are almost three houses away. We rub the water from our eyes and I see exactly where we are—outside of Sophie's house. Sophie is one of the meanest girls at our school. She wasn't always that way. Last summer she'd swim over to Nina's dock and play mermaid sisters. But she'd never do that now. To make things worse, Sophie's with her best friend, Amelia. They are sitting on Sophie's back porch. There's a plastic bucket between them and their legs are covered in white shaving cream. They take turns passing a razor back and forth. The razor leaves behind a stripe of shiny skin as it moves up their legs.

"Let's go back," says Nina. "They don't see us."

I nod. "Swim for as long as you can underwater. Don't come up until you have to."

But as I take a deep breath to fill my lungs, Sophie calls out: "Hey, Nina. Is it true that you're moving to New York City?"

Nina and I look at each other, trying to decide what to do. We could turn away and swim back to Nina's dock. We could fill our cheeks with water, run to the shore, and spit a long stream of Eel Pond right into their faces. But that's not the way it works with Sophie and Amelia. Their eyes are so steady they make us feel trapped, like we really are mermaids who've been caught in a net.

"I'm totally jealous," says Amelia.

"Me, too," says Sophie. "*Everybody* lives there. You'll probably run into tons of celebrities on your very first day."

"Maybe," says Nina.

Nina's legs slow. I don't know if she realizes that

she's drifting closer to shore. I have to paddle to stay by her side.

"And I bet you'll be super popular at your new school," says Amelia. "Everyone's going to think you're way exotic." Sophie bunches her eyebrows together, confused. But even from the water I can see something brewing in Amelia's eyes. Then Amelia says, "I mean, how else are you gonna explain the fact that you act like you're from a different planet."

"OMG," says Sophie, laughing. "Tell everyone you just moved from Planet Loser. They'll all love you! It's too bad you can't bring your pet dog Rover with you. That would complete the look perfectly."

Nina freezes. The water around her stills. Slowly her forehead drops under the surface, the ends of her hair floating above. There's a rocking from under the water. It hits my feet, my legs, my stomach. My arms lift as the water around me becomes choppy. I have to close my eyes because of the splashing. So I don't see the moment when Nina springs, but I feel its force.

When I open my eyes, Nina is on the shore.

She runs across Sophie's backyard and lifts the plastic bucket. I can tell it's heavy because Nina rocks back for a second before she raises it.

There is a moment when the foamy, dirty gray water floats in the air.

Then it lands in Sophie's and Amelia's laps.

And all I hear are screams.

4

"I can't believe you did that," I say.

"It just happened," says Nina. "Before I even thought about it. I hope I don't get in major trouble."

We are sitting on the dock. Nina hit the timer button on her watch as soon as we got out of the water and her eyes are fixed on the blur of digital numbers. She thinks if we can make it to ten minutes without Sophie and Amelia coming after us, then we're safe. I look across the water and back to Nina's house. Both are quiet. Clark must have given up on ringing the bell and gone inside.

"I don't think they'll tell," I say. "You drenched them in shaving water. It's gross. They won't want anyone to know."

Nina doesn't look up from her watch. "But they'll know that you know. What if . . ."

"I'll be okay."

"But the barking and everything."

The barking started last year when I came to school wearing a brown shirt the exact color of my hair. Sophie decided that I looked like a dog. Because in Sophie's head, that's the kind of thing that makes sense. Brown hair + brown shirt = dog. Sophie started calling me Rover and barking when I walked past. "Rover. Here, girl. Woof, woof."

"I'm so sorry I won't be there," says Nina.

"It's not your fault."

"Still."

We sit, looking out at Eel Pond. We make it to ten minutes. Then we hear: *Clang, clang, clang.*

Clark is standing by the bell, his hands on his hips. But he doesn't look mad. He's not shaking his head like he usually does when we don't come in after the first set of rings. Instead, Clark looks like he's trying to breathe everything in. Like if he could drink all of Eel Pond in a straw he would.

But he can't.

And neither can I.

"Your highness," says Toby as he pulls out my chair at the dinner table. He does a little bow, like I'm royalty. It's what Toby always does when I eat dinner at their house. It started a long time ago when Nina and I were obsessed with princesses. Back then, Toby was home a lot. He painted things like royal carriages, castles, and thrones on big pieces of paper that he hung on the wall outside his studio. Nina and I would play princess while Toby worked on his real paintings.

Toby knows we haven't played princess for years, so

I don't why he still does the pulling out the chair thing. I also don't know why it still makes me smile.

I sit down and look around their kitchen, trying not to see all the things that are different. Like the pile of serving plates in plastic bubble wrap. The slow cooker with its cord unplugged and wound in a coil like a snake. But my eyes keep finding more things. The teakettle with the rooster on top is gone. The shelf with the cookbooks is empty. The window seat no longer has pillows. More and more things are missing.

"All right, Cove," says Clark as he digs his fork into a plate of spaghetti and spins it. "You start."

I pick a gray marker from the glass cup in the center of the table. The game is that together, everyone at the dinner table makes a drawing. The first person draws until they lift the marker off the paper. Then they hand the paper to the next person. I don't know how Toby and Clark came up with this game, but we always play it when I stay for dinner. Being the first person is the hardest. You have to decide if you want to go big or small. Straight or loopy. Sometimes it's hard to decide. But tonight it's easy. I'm too sad about all the missing things to think of anything creative. Instead, I draw one straight gray line.

"Okay," says Toby as I hand him the paper. "Not your usual, but I can work with this." He takes a sip from his glass and grabs the same gray marker from the glass cup. He starts at the top corner of my line and continues it up, making a bunch of angles like a staircase. He draws a pointy top and goes back down, drawing a staircase in the other direction. By the time Toby's done, it's obvious what he's drawn—a tall New York City skyscraper. He's even made windows, all without lifting his marker. It's kind of cheating because the point of the game is to add to someone's drawing, not finish it. But Toby is such a fast drawer that sometimes he's almost done before the rest of us know what's happening.

Toby hands the paper to Clark. Clark picks a blue marker and turns the paper sideways, so that the skyscraper is laying on its side. Starting at the bottom of the skyscraper, Clark draws a wiggly line. Clark is not a good drawer, but it only takes a few seconds for us to realize that he's drawing the outline of Martha's Vineyard island around the skyscraper. When he's done, Clark hands the paper to Nina. Toby puts his hand on top of Clark's hand. He leans over to kiss Clark's cheek. They both look like they're about to cry.

Nina doesn't notice her dads because she's too busy grabbing the red marker. She grips the marker in all five fingers, like it's a hammer. Nina draws a huge X over the entire paper. She presses down hard, as if she is banging in a nail. "There," she says. "It's done."

Nina doesn't like to draw as much as I do, but she doesn't normally draw angry Xs at the dinner game. Usually she adds details, like long squiggly tongues on frogs and animal tails on alien people.

"Nina," says Toby, taking the paper away from her. "Sweetheart, please. Just give New York City a chance."

Nina shakes her head. "I don't want to give it a chance. I want to stay here. With Cove. We need to be together."

"I know you do," says Toby.

"No, you don't. You don't know anything. This is where we live. I'm staying."

Clark gets up and kneels next to Nina. "Martha's Vineyard is always going to be where we're from," he says. "Where we live isn't ever going to change that. We could live in Timbuktu and we'd still be from Martha's Vineyard. Does that make sense?"

"No," says Nina. "It doesn't make sense. Because we wouldn't be living here. We'd be living in Timbuktu. We'd be from Timbuktu."

Nina starts to cry. Part of me wants to reach for a marker and draw something silly like a dancing cupcake to cheer her up. But it's not the kind of crying that can just switch to laughter. So instead I say, "You'll be back soon. Like really soon, right?"

I look at her dads. They look at each other like they're both trying to think of the absolute perfect thing to say. That's when I start to get really worried. Because the perfect thing to say is: "Yes, Cove. Of course we'll be back soon." But that's not what happens.

"Listen, girls," says Clark. "When you're older you'll understand that being a family means you have to make compromises to support one another. Moving to New York City is a leap we have to take for our family. We'll need to see what happens."

"I don't need to see," says Nina, standing up from the table. "I already know that I'm going to hate it. Just like I hate you."

I was supposed to sleep over that night. Instead, Toby drives me home. There's still enough light to see the stone walls that line the winding roads in Chilmark.

Nina thinks the stone walls are like a 3-D puzzle, the way they fit together without cement. I've tried to look at the stone walls as a puzzle, but I never see them that way. I see the spaces in between the stones, where the edges don't fit together. Sometimes rays of light from the setting sun will shine through the cracks. The rays are sharp like icicles. They glow like flames. I used to pretend they were secret messages from fairies, signals only I could understand. Tonight, though, I look down at my lap. For all I care, it could be pitch-black.

"Sorry about dinner, Cove," says Toby as we get close to the turnoff for my house. "I think Nina just needs a good night's sleep. It's a lot to take in and all."

"Yeah."

"I'll bring her over tomorrow. You guys still have plenty of time together. We're not leaving for a few weeks."

The way he says it, I think Toby still thinks that Nina and I play princess outside his painting studio and hold imaginary tea parties with shells we found in the sand. He has no idea that sometimes all we do is talk. Just talk. About important stuff, like the bunny ears in the class picture, the book, and the girls who bark at me. Stuff that no one else in the world understands.

"And Cove, maybe once we get settled you could— " But Toby stops talking at the same time as he stops driving.

"What?"

Toby shakes his head. "Never mind, we're here."

Mom is waiting on the rocking chair on our front porch. Her tea mug is on the ground. She stands and wraps her arms around me. I put my forehead against the curve in her neck, where it's always warm. Mom smells like the lavender oil that she rubs on the inside of her wrists at night. I can tell by the way her chest moves that she's saying something to Toby. Mom and Toby have been friends for longer than Nina and I have been alive, but they still need to explain every single thing to each other. Not like me and Nina. Mom puts her hand over my ear, and I don't try to shift my head to listen.

It's nothing I want to hear.

5

The day Nina leaves, Mom drives us to the ferry in Oak Bluffs so that we can spend every last second together. We sit next to each other in the front seat of our truck and press our legs close. I notice the hair on our thighs, which I never have before. Nina's is light and mine is dark. The sun coming through the truck window makes uneven rectangular patterns on our skin, like the shapes in Toby's paintings of Nina. Only these shapes don't add up to anything at all.

When we pull up to the ferry dock, Nina's dads are waiting in the car line, their van stuffed full of their belongings. Duffel bags are pressed against the windows. Three bikes dangle from a rack. I feel sick, like when we hit a bump at the Artists Market and everything in my body lifts up, even my belly. Only this time I'm not floating. I'm sinking.

Nina and I link arms at the elbows. Our hold feels as strong as the bowline knot that Clark showed us when we were eight years old. "The king of sailing knots," he explained one day after school. "Something every true island girl needs to know." Clark gave us each a line of rope, singed at the ends, and taught us about the rabbit running through the hole, looping around the tree, and going back into the hole. When I got the hang of the knot before Nina, she threw her rope down and ran away.

I found her at the edge of Eel Pond. "Maybe I'm not a real island girl," Nina said as she threw stones into the water. But we both knew that wasn't true. We were island girls. Through and through. Still, I went over the bowline knot with Nina until she could do it with her eyes closed. But no matter how fast Nina got, she could never make the knot without mouthing the story about the rabbit and the tree.

Mom parks in a spot reserved for unloading passengers and turns off the truck. "Girls," she says. "I'm so sorry, but it's time."

"No," I say. "I'm not letting go."

"Me neither," says Nina.

"Well, then," says Mom with a fake sigh. "I guess I'll pick Cove up in New York City in a few days."

"Perfect," I say. "See you then." None of us laugh, but we all know it's a joke. Mom never leaves the island. So I never leave the island. Mom says that she's seen enough of the world to know that what matters most is what's inside your soul, and that her soul gets all the nourishment it needs on Martha's Vineyard.

Never leaving used to be okay with me.

But now, with the huge ferry waiting to take Nina

away, it's starting to not be okay anymore. There are so many summer people waiting to board. A few island people, too. Some people wait in cars, others stand in line on the dock. A couple carry only backpacks, but most group together next to piles of suitcases and take pictures with their phones. They point up at the seagulls circling overhead. They put their hands over their eyes to shade the sun. I can't tell if they look sad to leave Martha's Vineyard or excited. Where are all these people going? New York City? Timbuktu?

Toby walks up to our truck and leans his head through the open window. "Hey, girls," he says. "It's time to say good-bye now."

Mom closes her eyes and inhales through her nose. She steps out of the truck to give Toby a hug. They both start to cry. Toby squeezes Mom's arm. He leans close to her ear, as if he means to whisper, but since he's crying the words come out loud enough for me to hear. "We'd love to have you and Cove come visit anytime. Please think about it some more."

"Yes!" I say. "Yes! We'll visit."

"Cove," says Mom, wiping away tears.

"What? Toby wants us to."

"Not now, Cove. We'll talk about it later."

Toby nods and lets go of Mom's arm. "Come on, sweetheart," he says to Nina. "They're going to start loading the cars."

Nina's supposed to say no.

She's supposed to tighten her grip.

That was the plan we came up with this morning. Like when we were little and we'd hide under beds or inside closets whenever it was time for one of us to go back to our own home. I remember the pounding of my heart when we heard loud adult footsteps coming close. How it would be impossible not to giggle, as impossible as a balloon keeping in air once it's been pierced. Nina and I would hold each other tighter and tighter as the footsteps got closer and closer. As if the strength in our arms could stop the approach.

That's not what happens now.

"I have to go," Nina whispers. She wiggles her arm out of mine. Our legs separate, leaving a sticky patch of sweat behind. The seat shifts underneath me as Nina climbs out of the truck.

She puts her hand in Toby's hand.

She turns back to wave good-bye.

We are not as strong as a bowline knot after all.

"Oh, sweetie, it's not Nina's fault," says Mom as we watch them walk down the dock and get into their van. "She loves you very much."

"I know," I say.

And then I think something else. *It's your fault. It's your fault I'm being left behind. It's your fault I've never left this island.* The words feel like the Pop Rocks candies that Nina and I get from Candies from Heaven, the ones that explode inside your mouth when they hit your tongue. The words are exploding on my tongue, but I don't open my mouth to say them.

But I do remember one more thing about that afternoon when Clark taught us to tie a bowline knot. Right before I left to find Nina, Clark knelt down and looked me in the eyes, the way grown-ups do when they want to make sure you're really listening. "You have a creative mind, Cove," he said. "You pick up on things quickly. That's a true gift. Make sure you don't waste it. Don't let anyone hold you back." He paused then, as if he wanted to say something more but didn't know what words to use. "Just don't let yourself get stuck. You understand what I'm saying?"

Back then, I didn't understand. But now, as Nina's ferryboat motors off from the dock, away from the island I've never left in my entire life, maybe I am starting to.

6

At dinner I am quiet. I don't feel like talking. It's different being quiet at dinner when it's just me and Mom in our kitchen. When I'm quiet at other places, like at the Artists Market or dinner at Nina's house, it lets me see out better. I can watch the summer people as they shop with their families. I can listen to Toby and Clark tell stories about their day. There is so much noise around me that I don't notice I'm quiet. I don't notice myself at all.

But at home there's nothing to see except the plate in front of me. Nothing but the sound of my fork pushing the quinoa and kale salad around my plate. I don't push the food around because I think it's gross. The food my mom makes *sounds* gross—lentils, falafel, kimchi, chard, tofu. But when you've been eating it since before you had teeth, you get used to it. Sometimes you even crave it.

But other times, like tonight, you're just not hungry.

Mom pushes her plate to the side. She looks at the tattoo of my name on the inside of her wrist. She got the tattoo when I was a baby. "Have I ever told you the story of your name?" she asks.

I don't answer. She has told me the story of my name. She's told it to me one million times. But I still like hearing it.

Mom takes a sip of green tea. "So, there I was, with this tiny precious newborn in my arms. And it was the thirteenth day of the twelfth month in the conventional calendar, which is the ninth sign on the Zodiac calendar. That meant you were a Sagittarius, and Sagittariuses have a fire sign. They're passionate and strong and creative. I looked at you, and even though you were so teeny, I could tell that you were going to be all those things.

"But I also knew that fire signs do best when they have a place to feel safe. And that's when a vision popped into my head of a young girl standing in a deserted ocean cove. Waves were crashing all around her, but she was completely safe and at peace on her little stretch of sand. That's what I wanted for you. Always. So I named you Cove."

I smile. I can't help it. I like picturing my newborn baby self curled up in her arms. I like picturing that little girl standing on the sand. I even know what the girl is wearing—a red dress. It has a white ribbon tied around the waist, and the ends of the ribbon blow in the breeze. A matching ribbon holds back her hair.

"Did you ever worry that my name was too weird?" I ask.

Mom looks surprised. "Never," she says. "Never

ever. Your name's not weird. It's beautiful."

"But it's so different. I always have to say it twice. Like people can't hear it the first time."

"Cove, different is beautiful. You know that."

"Yes, but . . ." I don't know how to explain it to her. For the first time in my life, when I picture that little girl standing on the sand in her red dress, I realize that she doesn't look like me. Or, I don't look like her. Not anymore. I don't have her shiny brown hair tied back with a white ribbon. I don't have her big eyes and rosy cheeks. We're no longer the same person.

I don't how long it's been since we were.

"Cove Bernstein," I say.

"Well, the last name part wasn't my decision."

"Because it came from your parents. And their parents before them."

"Yes. But we've talked about this. It's just you and me now. We're all each other needs." She scoots back her chair. "You finished?"

As much as we talk about my first name, we never talk about our last name. Just like we don't talk about my dad. All I know is that he left before I was born and he's never coming back. And that sometimes the universe brings you gifts you never even knew you wanted. Gifts like me.

I wonder now if Mom watched my dad leave. Did she wave to him from the dock as he drove his car onto the ferry? Did she feel as sad as I feel? Why didn't she go with him? There are so many things I want to know, but one in particular that I *need* to know.

"Mom, please," I say. "Tell me why we never leave Martha's Vineyard."

"I've told you a thousand times, Cove. We're better off staying here." *Better. Stronger. Happier.* These are the words Mom uses whenever I ask this question. As if the words are complete answers, which they're not.

"Better off than what? I don't get what would happen if we left. Would we die? Is there some evil spell on us?"

"No, Cove. There's no spell. Well, not on you. But maybe there's one on me."

I know she doesn't mean an actual spell with a witch and a magic cauldron. But she looks so sad, her eyes on the table, that I feel scared anyway.

"Mom—"

"We've been through this, Cove."

"It's different now."

Mom opens her mouth as if she's going to ask me why it's different, but no sound comes out. She knows the answer. Mom runs her hand through her wavy hair, recrosses her legs. She sighs. "You know how Toby and Clark decided to move to New York City for the good of their family?" she says. "It's the same for us. We stay here, on this island, for the good of our family. This island is a safe place. I know who I am here. Out there, it's easy to get pulled under."

"And what, drown?"

"Yes, in a way. I don't want you to grow up the

way that I did. With the never-ending pressure to be a certain kind of person. With all the judgment. The expectations. It's toxic. Here, we can be different. We can be us."

"But we can be us anywhere," I say. "I promise."

Mom shakes her head. "You don't know what it's like other places."

"That's exactly my point!"

"See, Cove," says Mom. "You're already yelling. It's already starting. Just talking about leaving is changing the sacred atmosphere in our home."

Mom stands up and reaches for our plates. The tattoo of my name shows on her wrist. I want to grab a plate and throw it against the wall. Cause a crashing, shattering noise to break through the silence. But I stay frozen in my chair.

Mom puts the plates on the counter. She walks into her bedroom and closes the door.

The flowery scent of a burning candle drifts out.

Chanting music plays.

I go into my own room and close my own door.

I take out a piece of paper and begin to write Nina
a letter.

Dear Nina,

I hate my mom. I asked her again about leaving the island and she said no. Just like always. I want to climb out my bedroom window and never come back. I want to run all the way to Squibby, dive into the ocean, and swim far away.

Instead, I'm sitting in my same room, at my same desk, looking out at the same dark yard. I can't believe you just left this morning. It feels like it was ten years ago. But that doesn't make any sense because then we'd be babies. Is it weird to wish we were babies because then we'd still be together?

I'm imagining where you are as I write this. Are you still driving? Are you already in New York City? Wherever you are, I know you're somewhere I've never been. And even though I'm trying to picture what you're seeing, I'm sure I'm getting it all wrong.

Please tell me everything. What's New York City like?

Have you seen anyone famous yet? (Not that I think Sophie would be right about anything!) Do you like your new room? Have you been on the subway?

Write back as soon as you can. I'll check for letters every day.

Love,
Cove

P.S. This is a picture of how mad I am. Those are my eyes popping out of my face, in case you can't tell.

Dear Cove,

I'm sorry you hate your mom. I'm not so mad at my dads anymore, so maybe by the time you get this letter you're less mad at your mom, too.

NYC is awesome! The buildings are so tall! If you try to look all the way to the top, you get so dizzy that you feel like you're going to fall over. There's a park with an entire zoo inside and candy stores that are ten times the size of Candies from Heaven. Did you know that there are tons of colors of M&M's? They even come in purple! Don't you think it's stupid that they only put the boring colors in the regular packages?

We're staying in an apartment that belongs to someone who is in Africa studying gorillas. But we're going to find our own apartment soon. I like this apartment because the floor has black and white squares like a checkerboard. One night we played checkers right on the floor. I won. Like always!

Today we went to the gallery where they're going to show Papa's paintings. A girl who works there asked for my autograph. Like I was actually famous! Isn't that crazy? You have to tell Sophie and Amelia. Or maybe don't because I hate the idea of you going anywhere near them without me. Maybe write it on a note and slip the note in their backpacks when school starts. That way they'll know that I'm famous, but you won't actually have to talk to them.

I wish I could describe everything about NYC but there's too much. There are so many people. You can wear whatever you want and no one cares. I saw a boy on the subway with big silver spikes going all the way up his ear. That was pretty gross and I didn't really want to look, but then I couldn't stop looking.

I've been thinking that when I get my new room, I'm going to paint it light blue. I know I was going to do teal, but maybe blue will be better. Maybe it will remind me of Eel Pond.

Write back! I miss you!

Love,

Nina

P.S. Here's a terrible picture of me in front of a super-tall building. I look like an ant!

Dear Nina,

Breaking news—Delphina ran out of icies yesterday. It was so hot that her line ran all the way past Mom's table to Charleston's animal sculptures. The summer kids were sweaty and complaining, but Mom was happy because all those people stuck in front of her table meant she sold a lot of quotes. She said we can use the money to buy extra tickets at the Ag Fair.

Remember the Ag Fair last summer when we went on the Twirl-A-Whirl and we screamed so much that our throats hurt all night? And we thought we were going to puke after the first ride, but then we didn't so we decided to ride it two more times. Mom said she'd go on whatever rides I want, but I know she'll be too scared to go on the fun ones. She'd probably puke anyway.

There are only a few more Artists Markets left for the summer. That's good because I'm tired of sitting there with nothing to do, but bad because that means school's starting soon. I still can't believe you're not going to be at school. I wish I could send someone to New York City in your place. I'd send Amelia or someone like that. I guess that wouldn't be fair because then your dads would have to live with Amelia. But at least I'd have you back.

Tell me more about New York City. What else have you seen besides the spikes in that guy's ears?

Write back! I miss you!

Love,
Cove

P.S. Here's a picture of Delphina and her empty tub.

Dear Cove,

It's super hot here and I wish I could dive into Eel Pond. Remember the night we went swimming when it was dark and we pretended that the stars were space aliens? Then we freaked out and stayed up all night because we were so scared? Sometimes NYC feels like that. There are so many lights everywhere. I can see more lights from my bedroom window than all the stars over Martha's Vineyard. If I blink really fast, it looks like the lights are moving and I get totally freaked out. And you're not here to freak out with me, so I get bad scared instead of good scared.

But during the day it all makes sense and I kind of like it. We bought a huge map of the city and taped it to the fridge. I love how our neighborhood looks like it was drawn on graph paper. The streets make squares and most of the street names are numbers, so I can always tell where I am. Are you mad that I like it here? Don't be mad at me! I still miss you soooo much!

Write back!

Love,

Nina

P.S. Here's a picture of a space alien. Papa finished it for me at the dinner game. (Obviously)

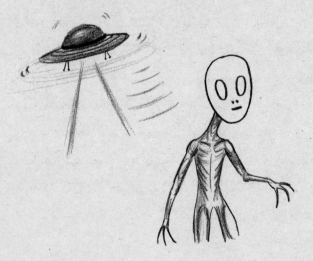

7

Nina has been gone for almost two weeks. Mom keeps talking about resilience, embracing the ever-changing universe, and the blessing of a skinned knee, whatever that means. But talking doesn't help. Nothing helps. I miss Nina just as much as the day she left. I know Mom is trying extra hard to cheer me up when she asks if I want to go back-to-school shopping before she has to teach yoga.

"Like at a store?" I ask.

Mom nods. "A store."

"Steffords?" Steffords is the biggest store on the island. They have circular clothing racks that spin.

They have an entire wall of shoes. I want Mom to say yes to Steffords so badly that I squeeze my eyes shut. Because I'm pretty certain she's going to say no, and I can't bear to see *and* hear the word at the same time.

"No," she says. "Sal's."

I knew it. "Please," I say, opening my eyes. "Just this once."

"Cove, you know how I feel about Steffords. They sell brands that manufacture their clothes in big factories. Those same brands make astronomical profits and don't pass any of the money down to the people who actually make the clothes. Do you really want to wear clothes like that on your body? Do you know what that would do to your spirit?"

"Make it happy because I'd actually be dressed like a normal kid?"

Mom inhales and presses her pointer fingers into her thumbs.

Sal's it is.

❦ ❦ ❦

Salvatore's Secondhand Shoppe is not the worst place, especially at this time of year when the summer people are cleaning out their houses and leaving Martha's Vineyard to go back to their real homes. Sometimes I'll get lucky and Sal will wait to sort a bag of clothes from a girl my size until I go through it. That's the best. Even though the clothes are usually crumpled up and stuffed into a paper bag, I like to see them all together. Then I can picture the girl who wore them.

If there are a lot of sports things, like mesh shorts and tank tops and fleece pullovers, then she's a girl with long hair pulled back into a ponytail. She bikes down North Water Street with her life vest zipped onto her handlebars. She laughs with her friends while they wait on the porch of the Edgartown Yacht Club for the launch to take them to sailing lessons on Chappaquiddick. If the clothes are more fancy, like skirts and patterned dresses, then she's a girl who takes art classes at the Old Sculpin Gallery and reads thick books on Fuller Street Beach in the afternoon. She rides her scooter to Mad Martha's ice cream at night and glides back home like a ballerina on wheels, all alone under the moonlight.

One time Sal left me a bag with a hand-knit poncho, drawstring pants, and flowing hippie shirts. It had cutoff jeans shorts and a few shirts in green and blue. Mom loved everything in it. But not me. I knew what kind of girl wore those clothes.

Someone just like me.

As we drive down the bumpy dirt road that leads from our house toward Beetlebung Corner, I think about what Nina wrote about the streets in New York City. Martha's Vineyard has North Road, Middle Road, and South Road. They all come together at Beetlebung Corner, but they're not straight or orderly. The roads on the island wind like old gnarly tree branches. They have names like Rumpus Ridge, Abel's Neck, and Wequobsque Road, not numbers.

Nina loves numbers. I wonder if she's standing on a numbered street right now, waiting to cross at a perfectly square corner. Does that make her happier than winding around Beetlebung Corner ever did? I wish I could call or text her to find out. Mom has a million reasons why she hates cell phones—radiation, government surveillance, distracted drivers, the big telecommunication companies. But as we turn onto South Road and I look out over the grassy meadows to the Atlantic Ocean, I feel so far from Nina. I would totally trade a little radiation for a chance to push some buttons and hear her voice.

Instead I hear our truck tires driving over crushed shells as we pull up to Sal's. "Go ahead, sweetie," says Mom. "I need to run a few quick errands. I'll meet you back here in a bit."

I open the door with the bell that tinkles overhead,

expecting to hear Sal call out, "Cove Bear!" Sal calls me Cove Bear because he thinks that everyone should have a nickname. Like Sal's full name is Salvatore, but everyone calls him Sal. Only there's no good nickname for Cove. But one day Sal saved me a shirt with a group of colorful smiling bears who looked like all they wanted to do was skip around making people happy. "These are the Care Bears," Sal explained. "They remind me of you, Cove. Spreading smiles wherever they go."

I wasn't allowed to wear the shirt, of course. "Too commercial," Mom said. "It turns you from a child into a walking advertisement for a television show." But Mom let me take the shirt home and keep it in my drawer. I could look at it whenever I wanted. And Sal decided that since *Cove* sounds kind of like *Care*, he would call me Cove Bear.

It's not that catchy, but it kinda stuck anyway.

When I don't hear my nickname, I figure Sal

must be in the back sorting clothes. So I start looking around. I head over to the shirt section. It's mostly button-downs and polos, not at all what I want. I'm searching for tank tops when I hear the words: "Up next, straight from New York City, we bring you a brand-new season of *Create You!*"

Sal's put a laptop on the counter next to the cash register. I stop looking through the clothes and start to watch the show that's playing on the screen. A tall woman wearing a green dress and hot pink high heels comes out from behind a curtain. She prances more than walks, lifting her feet with each step as if she's crushing a trail of ants. She is moving toward a group of teenagers. The teenagers bounce a little when she gets close, like they're so excited to see her that there's no way they can keep still.

"Welcome to *Create You*," says the woman. "I'm Martina Velez, cofounder of Velez Boyd Designs and one of your style gurus here on *Create You*. That means it's my job to guide you through the only competition that combines fashion and pure creative love. Are you ready to begin?"

"Yes!" all the teenagers cheer.

"Great," says Martina Velez. "First, I want to welcome you to New York City, where you will be living and designing for as long as you remain on *Create You*. How do guys like it here so far?"

They answer as a group, so it's hard to tell exactly what they say, but it's obvious that they love it.

Martina Velez leans back, like their happiness has physically moved her. She smiles and her teeth are so white that they glow on the screen. "Wow," she says. "I love you guys already. Now, before we begin our *Create You* journey, it's your turn to tell everyone who you are."

The ten teenagers say their names and where they're from. Carver, Jayce, Isobel, Paris, Eleanor, Alicia, Samantha, Kai, Harry, and Mika. They're from all over the country—Denver, Washington, Nashville,

Portland, Brooklyn, Philadelphia, and places I've never heard of like Encinitas and Kalamazoo. One boy has a streak of blue in his hair. One girl drew thick black lines around her eyes so they look like wings. I think about what Nina wrote in her letter, that everyone in New York City looks so different, and I smile because I feel closer to her. Like I get it more.

"Wonderful," says Martina Velez when they finish introducing themselves. "Now, are you ready to meet my cohost and design partner, Mr. Benjamin Boyd?"

I have no idea who Benjamin Boyd is, but everyone seems excited to meet him. They start looking around, as if he could appear from anywhere in the room.

"He's not coming to us," says Martina Velez. "We're going to him."

Suddenly the scene changes to a bald man wearing a black leather jacket and jeans. He's standing on a rooftop and looking at a door, as if he's waiting for someone to open it. When the camera moves to the door, I want to yell, "Stop! Go back!" I don't want to see the door. I want to see the view that flashed behind the bald man. The skyline of New York City.

I've seen pictures of New York City, of course. I've seen the tall-buildings pressed close together, the yellow taxis pouring down the crowded streets, the wide bridges, and the Statue of Liberty. But I haven't seen the city on TV since Nina moved there. It's silly, but part of me wants the camera to zoom down one hundred floors so I can look for her on the sidewalk. To see if maybe, just maybe, she's walking by.

"You watch?" asks a voice I don't recognize.

"Huh?" I say, turning around.

"The show? *Create You?* I'm tragically obsessed. It's the best reality show on TV by far. I've watched this episode twice already."

"So it's not live?"

"Negative. But don't worry, I won't spoil the ending for you."

I have no idea who this person is. And I would definitely remember if I'd seen him before. He's older than a teenager, but way younger than Mom. He's wearing tight black jeans with ripped knees. His hair is shaved on the sides and the middle is sculpted in spikes. The collar on his pink shirt is turned up, so he kind of looks like one of the preppy guys who sing a cappella on the street corners in the summer. The ones who wear their checkered shirts rolled up to their elbows and brown leather flip-flops with khaki shorts. But at the same time, he looks nothing like those guys. He seems to be working at Sal's, because he's got a collection of empty plastic hangers dangling from his wrist. He places the hangers next to a thick paperback book that is resting on the counter. The cover is bent and lots of pages are turned down in the corners.

"Who you rooting for?" he asks as he nods at the laptop. I must look as confused as I actually am, because he adds, "You know, to win."

"Oh," I say. "Um. Maybe Mika?" It's not a great answer because she's the one on the screen and her name is printed at the bottom. But he seems to go for it.

"Yeah, I can see it," he says. "She's got a cool boho vibe. I dig her caftan."

I have no idea what a caftan is, but I don't really care. I just want to keep watching the show. "Who's that?" I ask, nodding my head toward the bald guy who is still standing alone on the rooftop.

"Who, Benjamin Boyd? Come on, you've got to know Benjamin Boyd. He's the *man*. I mean, look at the way he rocks that bald head. It's like the dude was born to be bald. You can't write that kind of coolness with all the words in the dictionary. He and Martina Velez are fashion royalty. Their brand, Velez Boyd, is smoking hot right now."

"Right," I say. "Velez Boyd."

He looks at me like he's starting to understand that I have no idea what I'm talking about and that

I've actually never seen *Create You*. He pauses the show. "What's your name?" he asks.

"Cove," I say.

"Well, Cove. I'm Jonah. And you're obviously in desperate need of a *Create You* tutorial, like, stat." Jonah takes a deep breath. He runs his hand against one of his hair spikes. "Okay, so you've got Martina Velez and Benjamin Boyd. Think of them as the bosses of the show. At the start of every episode, they announce a design challenge. Like make an outfit out of an old pair of curtains or design a backpack featuring duct tape. That kind of thing. All the challenges involve some type of sewing. But most importantly, every challenge is supposed to represent *you*. The designer. Get it? *Create You?*"

I nod. "I get it."

"Okay, so then there are the contestants. They're chosen from all over the country to come to New York City and compete on the show. Everything's paid for.

Hotel, travel costs, the whole shebang." I picture the contestants smiling as they pull big suitcases through a fancy hotel lobby. I'm super jealous.

"But it's not all fun and games," continues Jonah. "The contestants work really hard. They get totally overwhelmed, they freak out, sometimes they cry, and Martina Velez and Benjamin Boyd talk them out of the depths of their despair. They give them advice on their designs before the contestants have to present what they've made."

"And then what?"

"At the end of every episode, they choose one winner and one loser. The winner gets immunity for a week; the loser goes home. And whoever's left at the end of the show wins a summer internship at Velez Boyd and a full scholarship to design school for college. It's major. Here, just watch."

Jonah restarts the show. Benjamin Boyd is speaking. "Okay, contestants," he says. "Your first design challenge will be to create one article of clothing that represents who you are on the outside and one article of clothing that represents who you are on the inside."

"And," adds Martina Velez, "you will be presenting them together as one complete look."

"I love these early challenges," says Jonah. "See how scared all the contestants look? Like their eyes are going to pop out of their heads. But then just wait. The stuff they make will blow your mind." He scrunches his hands into balls and then opens them wide, like a bomb exploding.

We sit and watch the entire episode. Jonah was right. Some contestants cry. Others freak out and pace around a big room that is filled with sewing machines and long tables. But in the end, they all create something. Ruffled tops paired with tight leather pants. Long dresses paired with woven metal bracelets. Sweatshirts paired with floral-patterned pants. When it's their turn, each contestant tells the stories that inspired their outfit. They talk about things that they're proud of and things they want to hide. About the people who make them feel ashamed and about the people who love them no matter what.

When the show ends, I have to blink and rub my eyes. Not because I'm crying, but because I feel like I've been transported somewhere else.

Somewhere bigger and more exciting than where I really am.

Somewhere close to Nina.

Dear Nina,

I just saw an awesome TV show called Create You. It's filmed in New York City! Have you seen it? It's about these teenagers who are competing in a design contest. A lot of the show takes place inside, but some parts happen outside. In the episode I saw today, there was a guy standing on the roof of a tall building. At the very end the camera zoomed all the way down to the sidewalk. And I totally got why the buildings make you dizzy. I felt like I had just stepped off the Twirl-A-Whirl. Remember how we walked all zigzag?

I loved the show because it felt like I was seeing the city in real life. Not like in a movie. At first I thought the show was live, but then Jonah said the show was filmed a few months ago. They film a new round of contestants every few months so maybe you'll see the new group. If you do, tell me everything because it would be cool to know who's going to be on the next season before anyone else.

I miss you! Write back!

Love,

Cove

P.S. Here's a drawing of a tall building in New York City. Did I get it right?

Dear Cove,

I promise I'll look for the people on Create You! But it might be hard because when they film movies and TV shows there are usually ropes so people walking by can't get too close.

Also the city is so big! My dads got Fitbits because we walk so much and they have a competition to see who can get the most steps in one day. When one of them is close to a big number like 7,000 or 8,000, he lets me put his Fitbit on my wrist. It's fun to watch it change to the perfect number. But then I never want to take the next step because that ruins everything.

The buildings don't make me feel dizzy anymore. I guess I'm used to them.

Love,
Nina

P.S. Who's Jonah?

Dear Nina,

Oops! Jonah is working at Sal's because Sal is off island for a few weeks. He's super nice. Jonah brought his laptop to the store and that's how I saw Create You. I can't wait to go back and watch some more.

I wish you could meet Jonah. I think you would like his hair.

Love,
Cove

P.S. Here's a picture of Jonah's hair.

Dear Nina,

Did you get my letter about Jonah? Are you mad at me? I didn't mean he's nicer than you. He's nothing like you. You're my best friend. I miss you! Please write back!

Love,
Cove

September

8

Twice a week Mom teaches paddleboard yoga on Sengekontacket Pond. In the beginning of the summer she hangs posters all over the island that have a picture of her in downward dog on a paddleboard. The sun is setting between her arms and legs, so it looks like she's bending over a ball of fire. People stop and stare at those posters. They say, "I want to do that." And I get it. There's something about the picture that makes Mom look like an enchanted warrior woman who has captured the sun with her powers. Maybe that's why so many people come to her class. Because they can't help but wonder if there's something magical about her. And if the magic will spread to them.

Sometimes, when I look at the picture, I wonder the same thing.

But I also know the truth: that Mom thinks it's silly to do yoga on a paddleboard in the middle of a pond. I've seen what actually happens when the same people who stared at the poster lie down on their stomachs and make their way to the middle of the water. The wobbling begins as soon as they try to stand. It only takes a few minutes before they tumble. But no matter how many times they fall, Mom always says something that makes them smile.

Making all those people smile must be tiring, though. Because as she pulls into a parking spot Mom whispers, "Last class, you can do it." And I feel a little bad for her. I lean over and give her a hug. It's supposed to be a quick hug, but then she puts her nose against my hair and inhales. It makes me feel like a baby when

Mom smells my hair, but it also makes me feel safe. I run my finger over the seat of our truck until she kisses me on the forehead and pulls away.

"You're such a blessing," she says. "I don't know what I'd do without you."

"Okay," I say.

While Mom teaches yoga, I'm supposed to wait on the Sengekontacket beach or across the street, where I can watch people jump from the Jaws Bridge. The Jaws Bridge got its name because it was part of a movie about a shark attack. I haven't seen the movie, but it made Martha's Vineyard famous. Everyone who lives here knows the movie wasn't about a real shark. The director made a fake shark and sent it swimming through the water with really scary music playing in the background.

But still, part of the fun of jumping off the Jaws Bridge into the waters of Nantucket Sound is thinking that maybe, just maybe, there's a real shark waiting in the water. Nina and I used to do it all the time. We'd stand on the rickety wooden bridge, gripping the railing with our toes, and count to however old we were. I know you're supposed to count to three, then jump, but three just isn't long enough. Because the best part is that moment when your knees are bent and you're holding hands and your eyes squint because the sun is shining off the water and you know you're about to fly.

Most of the kids on the bridge today are summer kids, probably taking their last jumps of vacation before they get on the ferry at Oak Bluffs. I can tell because they stand on the railing for way too long and pose for pictures. Sometimes they shout as they work up the courage to jump. It's fun to watch them almost lose their balance. One boy falls before he's ready, his arms making wild circles like a windmill at full speed.

I'm laughing to myself when I hear it. It drifts over the screams and the sound of splashing water. "Woof, woof. Hey, Rover."

My heart sinks.

"Yoo-hoo, Rover. Over here, girl."

They are standing on the other side of the bridge, waving their fingers like dainty princesses. Sophie is wearing a neon-pink bikini with black trim around the edge. She has her right foot tucked into the thigh of her left leg, like she's in a yoga tree pose. Amelia has large sunglasses over her eyes, and her arms are crossed in front of her chest. The glitter case on her phone is sparkling in the afternoon sun.

There are so many people in between us, but there may as well be none.

Because they are together and I am alone.

I've been thinking about this exact moment, wondering what I would do when it happened. Not *if* it happened. *When*. Because after Nina threw the dirty shaving water all over them, there was no chance Sophie and Amelia would let me out of their evil grip. No way I would be just Cove to them.

But no matter how much I've thought about this moment, I still don't have a plan for what to do. I need to make a decision. *Fast.*

I can pretend that they aren't actually barking at me and hope they get bored.

I can tell them to stop in a loud clear voice like the lady at the anti-bullying assembly. "Stop," she yelled as she raised her hand in front of her, palm facing out. "I'm asking you to STOP." Then her pretend bully, a boy named Sam who she picked from the audience, put his hands over his head and shuffled away, wiping pretend tears from his cheeks. Everyone cheered at Sam's performance. Because that's what it was—a performance. It's not the way things work in real life.

I can cross the street and swim to Mom. Dive into Sengekontacket Pond in all my clothes and let the salt water wash away the tears that I can feel building. But Mom's in the middle of teaching her class. And Sophie and Amelia would probably just watch and laugh.

None of these options is good.

In this moment, only one seems to stand a chance.

So I take it.

"Hi," I say as Sophie and Amelia walk toward me. I don't want to say it. Saying it makes me want to curl up in a tiny ball. But I force myself.

"What are you up to, Roves?" asks Amelia. She says it super friendly, which makes it sound super mean.

"Nothing," I say. *Pretend it's not happening. Maybe they'll get bored.*

"Oh, right," says Sophie. "Because your BFF Nina left you to move to New York City. I totally forgot all about that."

"That's right," says Amelia, hitting her forehead with the hand that's holding her phone. The phone dances a little in her fingers.

"Don't drop it," I say.

"Drop what?" asks Sophie.

"The phone."

They both laugh. "It doesn't work that way, Rover," says Amelia. "It's not, like, slippery."

"I just meant . . ." I don't know what I meant. I was only trying to come up with something to say. Trying to stick to the best option. I try again. "What are you guys doing?"

"Just looking at some clothes," says Amelia. "On Amazon."

"She means the website," says Sophie. "Not the jungle."

"I know," I say. Martha's Vineyard is a small island, and everyone knows about my mom and how she won't let me buy anything from Steffords, or online. And everyone knows that Amelia's mom is one of the top real-estate agents on the island and that she lets Amelia buy any kind of clothes she wants, from wherever she wants.

"I hope the shirts come before school starts," says Amelia.

"Totally," says Sophie. "They're going to be perfect for the first day."

I glance at the phone and see an image of a white shirt with black writing. But with the glare of the sun, I can't make out the words. "What do they say?" I ask.

"You'll have to wait and see," says Amelia.

"OMG, I just thought of something," says Sophie. "If we order the shirts today, they'll be here for the back-to-school picnic on Saturday. Twinsies?"

"Twinsies!" says Amelia. They squeal and clap. For one flickering moment, I really do think that Amelia is going to drop her phone into the water. But she doesn't. Girls like her never do.

The back-to-school picnic. I am dreading the back-to-school picnic. It's called a picnic because everyone is supposed to bring food and eat outside on the picnic tables by the playing fields. But it's really more of a dance, with music and stuff.

"What are you going to wear to the picnic, Cove?"

asks Amelia. "I'm sure you have something ravishing all picked out."

Sophie fidgets with her hair. It's braided in a messy side ponytail that reminds me of Mika from *Create You*. So maybe that's why I answer, "I don't know. Maybe a caftan."

"A caftan? What's a caftan?" asks Sophie. She wrinkles her nose as if the word smells bad.

And I realize I have absolutely no idea.

Luckily, three older girls jump from the Jaws Bridge. They scream so loudly that everyone turns to watch. One girl is even screaming as she hits the water. It makes me think about the whales we learned about last year in science. About how some of them can hear one another up to one thousand miles away. I wish my voice could travel through the ocean waters all the way to New York City.

Then I would say to Nina: "You have to come back. I can't do this without you."

9

A jetty of rocks runs from Menemsha Beach into the ocean. Mom and I go there to watch the sunset. Sometimes there's a man who makes enormous bubbles from a rope that he dips into a bucket of soapy mix. The man never says a word, not even to the little kids who stand right beside him. He just dips and waves his rope, watching as the translucent shapes float away, the colors of the rainbow reflected on their invisible skin.

"It reminds me of an offering," Mom says that evening as we watch the bubble man. "Do you see that, Cove? He's offering something of great beauty into the sky."

"What does he think he's going to get back?" I ask.

"Well, nothing. The point isn't the getting. The point is to make something of beauty and release it into the world. The joy is in the creating, not the receiving. Just ask any great artist."

"Like Toby?"

She smiles. "Yes, exactly. Like Toby. I bet if you asked him, he would agree with me."

"So why don't I?"

"Why don't you what?"

"Ask Toby," I say. "I've been thinking. Why can't I go to New York City by myself? Toby and Clark wouldn't mind. They always love it when I sleep over. They—"

"No," Mom interrupts. "No way."

"Why not?"

"New York City is far, Cove. Flights off island are hundreds of dollars. And let's say you took the ferry to Woods Hole, then what? Are you going to get a bus to

Boston and then switch to a second bus to New York City? Or a train? You're not a bubble, Cove. I'm not just going to send you into this enormous world all alone."

"Because you think I'll pop? That makes no sense."

"It might not make sense to you, but it makes sense to me. We can talk about it when you're older. But not now."

"Please, Mom. I'm not a bubble. Look." I yank on my hair. I pinch the skin on my arm. "I can do it. I'll be fine. Please." Tears form in my eyes. Not from the yanking and the pinching, but from everything else. The post office box that is stuffed with bills and catalogues, but no new letters from Nina. The barking. The end-of-summer chill in the air. The countdown of days until school starts. The sand stuck between my toes, the seagulls swooping over my head, the jetty underneath me, all of them reminding me that Mom's right: I am very far away from New York City.

Mom puts her arm around my shoulders. She kisses my cheek as she looks out at the water. A man walks across the beach with a paddleboard balanced on his head. He puts the board on the sand by the water's edge and takes off his shirt. He has tattoos up and down his arms, but he's too far away for me to see them clearly. The man steps onto the board, looks in our direction, and waves. My mom waves back. She sits up a bit straighter.

"Do you know him?" I ask.

She nods. "His name is Sean. He's been coming to my yoga classes and sometimes we talk afterward. I think you'd like him. Do you want to say hi?"

"Since when do you care about what I want?"

"Cove, that's not fair."

"Why not? It's true."

Mom stands and brushes sand from her jean shorts. I let her take a few steps, then I follow. We step from rock to rock, making our way to the beach. Mom moves farther ahead, skipping over a few rocks. When she reaches Sean, she lifts onto her toes and kisses him on the cheek. He pulls her close with one arm and she laughs.

I stop walking.

Mom's gone on dates before. I would sleep over at Nina's house and Mom would get me the next morning, collapsing onto the padded window seat in the kitchen as Toby and Clark sat on either side and listened to the story of her date. Mom never knew, but Nina and I would listen, too. We'd sit on the back stairs, pressed tight against the wall, giggling with our hands over our mouths as Mom told stories of horrible kisses and guys who spit food when they talked.

"Do you want your mom to have a boyfriend?" Nina asked one morning.

I shook my head. "No. Gross."

We laughed, but I was serious. I had Nina. Mom. Toby and Clark. Someone else, one of the slobbery kissers or food spitters, would mess everything up. I was glad that her dates were all awful. But Sean does not look like the men Mom used to describe. No beard. No round belly. Mom laughs at something Sean is whispering in her ear. She whispers something back.

Mom believes in Karma; the idea that what you put into the universe, the universe gives you back. Maybe on all those dates Mom didn't want a boyfriend. Maybe her Karma was telling the universe that we had enough. Both of us. And now, her Karma is telling the universe that we don't.

"Cove," calls Mom, waving. "Come on. This is Sean."

I can't stay on the rocks all night. Slowly I walk in their direction.

"What's up, Cove," says Sean when I reach them. He raises his hand to give me a high five. "I've heard so much about you."

"Hi," I say. Mom looks as if she wants me to

continue, or at the very least slap Sean's hand. But what am I supposed to say? I look down at the sand and dig a hole with my big toe.

Is Karma something you need to be old enough to have? Like a driver's license? Because I have been asking the universe for a way to see Nina since the day she left. So far I've gotten nothing back. Nina is still in New York City. I am still here. And I have no idea when I'll see her again.

However Karma works, it doesn't work for me.

But that night, I have a dream.

I am standing in New York City. The streets are a perfect grid, just like Nina described. It's daytime, but no one else is around. I search for someone to explain what is happening. As I turn my body, I feel a weird swishing movement. I am wearing a long gold skirt. It glimmers like the sun on Mom's paddleboard yoga posters. I touch my stomach and feel the fuzziness of a hand-knit sweater. Then hands start to clap from somewhere in the distance. I follow the sound and see Martina Velez and Benjamin Boyd. They are walking toward me from across the empty street. "Congratulations, Cove," says Benjamin Boyd. "Welcome to *Create You*."

"Let's take a walk, shall we?" says Martina Velez.

We walk down the middle of the street, following the yellow divider lines like they're a balance beam. I catch a glimpse of myself in the windows of a tall building. My feet are bare under my long skirt. I wave at my reflection, but my reflection does not wave back.

"Come along, Cove," says Benjamin Boyd.

"Someone's expecting you," says Martina Velez.

Suddenly I wake up.

I wiggle my toes, hoping to feel concrete, but feel a tangle of sheets instead. I close my eyes and try to get the dream back. But it's gone. All that's left is a feeling that I was actually in New York City. And that the person waiting for me was Nina.

10

Mom is in a handstand when I come into the kitchen for breakfast. She pushes off the wall with her toes, her long legs opening like scissors, and stands upright with her hands on her hips. "Hey, sweetie," she says. "Good morning."

I reach for a grape from the bowl on the counter. "Can I go to Sal's today?" I ask. After my dream last night, I really want to watch *Create You* again. And there's only one place I can do that.

"Again? But we just bought you some clothes. That feels a bit excessive to me."

"I don't want to shop," I say. "It was so messy in there last time. I think Sal could use some help. With the sorting and stuff."

"Oh, well, that's a very kind thought. But did Sal say this was okay? I didn't get a chance to talk to him last time we were there."

"I'm sure he won't mind," I say, pausing. "I don't know, it would just be nice to have something to do before the back-to-school picnic. That way I won't have to spend all day alone."

That gets her, just like I knew it would. Mom knows I've been dreading the back-to-school picnic. My first school event without Nina. "I teach at ten thirty," she says. "How about we swing by Sal's on the way."

Mom drops me at the front door. We had to stop for gas, so she's worried about being late to her class and doesn't come inside. "I'll be back in a few hours," she says. "Be good for Sal, okay?"

I nod and wave good-bye as I push open the door with its tinkling bell. Jonah is sitting on the counter underlining something in a thick book. His hair is different today, in one smooth wave instead of spikes.

"Cove," he says. "Covester, the Covinator, you're back."

"Yeah," I say. "Is that okay?" If I wasn't holding the door open I would be crossing my fingers, because it occurred to me on the way over that maybe Jonah doesn't want me to hang around all day. Maybe he was just being nice to me before because he was bored.

"Of course, it's okay," he says. "This place is *d-e-a-d* dead and this book is *d-e-n-s-e* dense. I was hoping for some fabulous company, and it looks like my wishes have been granted."

I smile, relieved. There's no one else in the store. Clothes hang still on the racks, random sleeves and skirts poking out as if they're looking for extra attention. I've taken a few steps toward the back, as if I might start browsing, when Jonah asks, "You have time for some intense *Create You* action?"

We watch three *Create You* episodes in a row.

We eat two bags of Swedish Fish.

We pause for one bathroom break.

The bell over the door does not ring once.

By the end, I not only understand the show, but also the contestants. I get who they are and what their style is. I even have my favorites.

There's Carver from Kalamazoo. His name sounds hard and sleek, but he's just the opposite. He's got a round face covered in pimples. Carver says that where he lives, all the boys are supposed to play football and soccer. But he hates sports. So his parents would leave him home with his grandmother while they took his brothers to all their practices and games. Carver's grandmother taught him to sew. He describes his style as refined and elegant, just like her. When Carver talks about his grandmother, he tears up. She died just a few months ago.

There's Paris from Brooklyn, which is kind of confusing. She's awesome and super tough. Paris never tears up, not even when the judges say her outfit for the "Future You" episode is a total bust. She's all about metal and spikes and lots of slits. Benjamin Boyd and Martina Velez suggested that Paris incorporate some color into her designs, but she didn't take their advice. Paris says that texture can express more than any color in the world. But she does dye the tips of her hair neon pink, so I'm not sure she totally believes that.

Alicia from Ohio is shy in front of the camera. But when she's designing, with her mouth full of pins and yards of fabric spread out on her worktable, she sings to herself and seems to have no idea that anyone can hear. Her style is more retro, with full skirts and tight tops that button up to the neck. She likes to make flowers out of fabric and pin them onto her outfits.

But my favorite by far is Mika. The girl from California. Mika loves color and pattern and mixing it all together in flowing layers. A lot of her designs have cutouts in places you would never expect. Like down just one arm or across the lower back. When she's nervous, Mika chews on the ends of her long black hair. But it's not gross, because nothing Mika does is gross. She's the coolest girl I've ever seen.

At the end of our third episode, Jonah stands up and starts to close his laptop. "Please," I say. "Just one more episode."

"Man, you're quite the super fan," says Jonah. "I appreciate your dedication to worshipping at the altar of *Create You*. So one more episode. One! But then you're cut off, okay?"

"Okay," I say. I'm about to ask if Jonah has any more Swedish Fish when the bell over the door sounds. An old woman wearing a gray cardigan sweater with polished wooden buttons walks into the store. Her white hair is tied back in a neat bun.

Jonah slams the laptop shut. "Welcome to Salvatore's," he says. "Let me know if I can be of assistance." He winks at me and starts to fold a pile of T-shirts that have been sitting on the counter all morning.

As the woman moves toward the back of the store, I walk to the counter. I rip a piece of paper from the notepad by the register and grab the pen that was next to Jonah's book. I draw something every single day—flowers, tiny alien people with huge eyes, squiggly patterns that repeat at different angles. But I've never drawn a fashion sketch like the contestants draw on *Create You*. The kind that looks like the drawing could walk right off the page. I wonder if I could.

I lower the pen to the paper. I loosen my grip and bend my wrist. Carver starts his sketches with long strokes that form legs and arms. Mika keeps her pen super light at first, making darker lines as she goes on.

So that's what I try to do. I don't know how much time passes before I feel Jonah looking over my shoulder.

"What do we have here?" he asks.

I put my hand over the paper. "Nothing," I say. "It's not done."

"It doesn't look like nothing. It looks like a sketch directly inspired by a certain fabulous TV show."

"Really?" I move my hand from the paper. I notice every wrong angle and messed-up line. An arm that looks like a snake. A head that looks like a floating balloon. Before I can cover the drawing back up, Jonah grabs it and holds it at arm's length.

"Huh," he says, tilting his head and scrunching his lips. "This is relatively awesome, Cove. It's totally like what they draw on *Create You*."

"You think so?" I tilt my head like Jonah's. From this distance, my sketch does look a lot less terrible.

"Dude, I know so. You should give it a shot. Dream the impossible dream."

"What dream?" I say. But I know what he's talking about—*Create You*. I know because as I was drawing, two thoughts flipped back and forth in my brain. *What if I could get on* Create You? *No, there's no way. What if? No way. What if? No way.*

Jonah puts the drawing on the counter and raises both eyebrows.

"You mean get on *Create You?*" I say.

"Not just to get on *Create You!* To win the whole darn thing!" Jonah turns in a circle, his arms flung wide. I can't tell if he's being serious or making a joke, but I suddenly feel very serious.

"But how?" I ask. "How would I do it?"

Jonah shrugs. "No clue. Why? You actually want to go for it?"

"My best friend moved to New York City. My mom won't let me go visit her. But if I find a way to go on my own, my mom won't be able to stop me. You said the show pays for everything, right? Travel and hotel and all that." The words spill out before my brain completely understands them. But once they're out, floating in the air between me and Jonah, there's no way to take them back.

"Huh," says Jonah. "A long-lost best friend is what I call a serious conundrum in desperate need of a solution. Thankfully, we've got the internet. Let's see what we can find out." Jonah checks to make sure the old woman is still in the changing room and opens his laptop. He goes on the *Create You* website and clicks on the "Become a Contestant" link. His head rocks side to side as he scrolls. "*Create You* is looking for the future of blah, blah, blah . . . Let your unique voice blah, blah, blah . . . New York City blah, blah, blah."

He stops scrolling. "Okay, here. This is what we need. It says, 'In order to be considered for candidacy, all applicants must submit a statement of purpose and an original article of clothing designed and sewn by the applicant. Applicants whose designs meet our criteria will be invited to participate in an on-air screen test before final selections are made. All applicants must be between twelve years of age and seventeen years of age at the time of submission. Applications are reviewed in the order in which they are received."

"You're under seventeen years of age, I presume?" says Jonah.

I smile. "Yes, I'm twelve."

"Phew. So you've got the age thing working for you. And we know you're a great artist. Any clue how to sew?"

I shake my head.

"Any ideas for how to learn?"

"No."

"Well, then, I would say you've got your work cut out for you. I can't help you with the sewing part, but I do love fashion. And I'm a *Create You* expert. I'll teach you everything I know."

I wait in the parking lot for Mom. I don't want her
to go inside and realize that Sal's off island. She
would want to talk to Jonah. Find out how we spend
our time at Sal's. "Watching a television show about
clothing?" I imagine her saying. "Is that really the best
use of your limited time on this planet?"

So I hop into our truck as soon as Mom pulls up.
Her hair is hanging in loose curls around her face.
Her wrists are stacked with her favorite bracelets.
She's meeting Sean, the paddleboarder with the
tattoos, this afternoon. I saw it written on her

calendar right next to "Cove School Picnic."

"Did you have a nice time with Sal?" she asks.

"Yep," I say.

"Excited for the picnic?"

"Nope."

Mom sighs. "This could be your best school year ever, Cove. Stay open to the possibility. I believe in you. I believe that wonderful things are waiting for you."

Mom could keep this up for the entire drive. I need to change the subject. "Do you know how to sew?" I ask.

"I can barely knit."

"Do you know how I could learn? Are there classes I can take?"

"I've never seen a sign for classes, but I'll ask around. In return, you need to sign up for something at school. Like an afternoon club or something."

"A club?"

"Something to help you expand your horizons."

Something to help you make friends. That's what she

really means. "Fine," I say. "But only if I can also learn to sew."

"Agreed," says Mom. But from the way she smiles and pats my leg, I can tell she's not concerned with keeping her end of the deal. I look out the window, my mind spinning like the wheels of our truck. Does Jonah seriously think I should apply to *Create You*, or was he just making a joke? What would it be like if I actually got accepted? How would it feel to walk down the streets of New York City? But then the school building comes into view and my thoughts shift from wonder to dread. I have no idea who I'm going to sit with at the picnic. How I'm going to survive the picnic. How I'm going to survive school. These thoughts drop from my brain to my stomach. I worry that they're going to explode and splatter all over the truck.

I've driven past school all summer long. There's no way to avoid it. But when we drove past in the summer, I could look the other way, to the skate park across the street. Now, as Mom pulls into the entry circle and stops next to the flagpole, there's nowhere else to look but the glass double doors with "Martha's Vineyard Middle School" written above.

"Don't forget your food," says Mom as I open the door.

"Mom, I told you. It's just called a picnic. No one actually eats."

"The letter from Principal Finnery specifically said to bring food."

"Fine, I'll take it. But I'm not going to eat it."

"Cove, you know how I feel about that kind of wasteful attitude toward—" She stops. Takes a deep breath. "I know it's going to be hard this year without Nina. But there are so many girls in your grade. Maybe it will be nice to make some new friends. What about that girl Charlotte?"

"Which one?" There are two Charlottes in my grade. Charlotte M. lives on a horse farm in West

Tisbury and fills her notebooks with doodles of horse heads. She's actually pretty good. And horses are not easy; I've tried. The problem is Charlotte M. also likes to gallop between classes. She closes her eyes, grabs imaginary reigns, and takes off down the hall with her backpack bouncing. Some kids neigh as she passes, but Nina and I never did. It felt too much like barking.

The other Charlotte, Charlotte L., is kind of friends with Sophie and Amelia, but she mostly hangs out with the girls on her dance team. She always has a pack of bubble gum tape in her backpack, the kind that comes out in a long strip with a sugary smell that you can almost taste. Charlotte L. likes to break off pieces of gum for her friends, then lean back and dangle the biggest piece of all into her own mouth.

"The one who always has bits of hay in her hair," says Mom.

"That's Charlotte M.," I say. "She only wants to hang out with horses."

"Okay then. The other one."

"Charlotte L.?" I roll my eyes. "No way."

"Why not?"

Where do I start? How do I explain to Mom, who believes that each person has a divine spirit inside of them that shines in its uniquely wonderful way, that it's not as easy as *me* wanting to be friends with *them*. It's not like our spirits jump out of our bodies and hug. There's other stuff, on the outside. There's the clothes other girls wear that are clingy and colorful. The bra straps that peek through their tank tops and the fringed bikinis they wear on the beach. The phones they hold in their hands and the backpacks they carry on one shoulder, dangling keychains bouncing up and down with every step. There are the songs they listen to through shared headphones, the pictures they post online, and the videos they watch on YouTube.

There are layers and layers of things. Even if Mom thinks that stuff doesn't matter, it does.

The only person it didn't matter to was Nina. But she's not here anymore. She's not on this island. She doesn't go to this school. She's not at this stupid picnic.

It's just me.

So I go.

Alone.

I walk around the brick building to the playing fields. From this side I can see my old elementary school. The playground where Nina and I raced to the swings so we could be first on at recess. The sandbox where Matt Lebeki peed in kindergarten and Mr. Rambos, the school janitor, had to shovel the sand into a trash can and bring in a fresh truckload from way out on Cape Poge. I always wondered where Mr. Rambos took the old peed-on sand. Probably South Beach, where the summer people love to boogie board in the waves.

I pass the window to Ms. Bard's first grade classroom. In first grade we studied geography, and I realized how many different kinds of places there are in the world. Urban. Suburban. Rural. We had a long debate about what Martha's Vineyard was. Some kids thought it was urban because it has three separate towns. Others thought it was suburban because of the neighborhoods of houses with big yards and bike paths. Most thought it was rural because it has so much rolling farmland and it's hard to get to.

Then I raised my hand. "It's everything," I said. "Everything all in one place and that's why it's so special." Ms. Bard clapped her hands together and I felt proud, like I had figured out something difficult. But now I know better. Martha's Vineyard is just an island. A piece of land floating in the great big Atlantic Ocean far away from everything else.

I place my bag of food near a side door and walk toward the picnic. Mr. Turner, the gym teacher, is standing behind a folding table and DJing music from his phone. But no one is dancing. A group of boys are playing at the four-square court, pushing one another as they wait in line and making farting noises with their hands. One boy who I've never seen before is watching the four-square game from a distance. He takes his hands in and out of the pockets of his jeans, like there's something inside that he needs to check is still there.

Some girls are sitting at the wooden picnic tables handing tubes of lip gloss back and forth. They pull the wands out of the containers, holding the goopy, glittery sticks up to the light before applying them to their lips. Charlotte L. is with those girls, three wands spread in her hands as if she's playing go fish and debating her next move. If only Mom could see her now.

I have to figure out where to go. I can't just stand here. So I try to look around without looking like I'm looking around, which is kind of impossible and makes me regret leaving my food at the door. Opening a bag of kale chips would at least give me something to do.

Sophie and Amelia are off to the side near Mr. Turner. Sophie is standing in her normal tree pose, with her right foot tucked into her left thigh. Amelia is next to Sophie braiding the ends of her hair. Standing with them are Molly and Caroline. Molly and I were partners in theater class last year. We had to pretend to be cats, crawling around stage on our hands and knees. Then Molly got a thumbtack stuck in her hand, and the teacher asked me to walk her to the nurse. Molly cried and squeezed my hand while the nurse poured rubbing alcohol onto her cut. She squeezed so hard that her fingers left white prints on my palm. I wish I could walk over to Molly. But I can't. It's like the other girls are a huge stone wall, way too big to climb over.

Still, I start to move closer. Not close enough that they'll notice me, but close enough that I don't look like I'm standing all alone. I'm trying to decide exactly where to go when their group shifts. Their heads move closer into a huddle and their shoulders shake a little from giggling. Sophie switches legs, so that now she's balancing on her right leg with her left foot tucked into her thigh. Amelia unbuttons her jean jacket. Caroline fiddles with the zipper to her sweatshirt. Molly looks over her shoulder.

"One, two, three," says Amelia. "Do it!"

All four girls take off their top layer at the same time. Underneath they're wearing matching white shirts with black writing. The shirts from Amelia's phone. They're hugging one another and jumping up and down, so at first it's hard for me to read the words. Then I read them perfectly: STAY AWAY FROM US.

I freeze, unable to take another step. Sophie and Amelia stick their chests forward, as if they're trying to make the letters look bigger. Caroline holds her zip-up sweatshirt by her side and looks down at the grass. Molly bites the side of her lip. I can't move. But I also can't look away.

Amelia notices me. "What?" she asks, smirking.

I shake my head. "Nothing."

"Thought so," she says.

"Come on," says Sophie, linking her arm in Amelia's. "Let's find a table. I brought Doritos."

They walk past me and sit at a wooden picnic table near Charlotte L. and those girls. Molly and Caroline follow. At first it seems like the only other person who noticed what just happened is the boy with his hands in his pockets. Which makes sense because he's the only other person standing alone. He rolls his eyes. He kicks the grass with the toe of his boot. Mr. Turner puts on a different song, this one with a faster beat. The boys shove one another in the four-square line. The girls pass their lip gloss.

But then, slowly, things start to get quiet. The teachers who had only minutes before been standing and laughing in tight groups, arms crossed and glasses dangling from chains around their necks, begin to tap one another on the shoulders. The thud of the ball hitting the cement four-square court stops. Mr. Turner turns off the music, as if maybe that will help him to understand what's going on. Sophie, Amelia, Caroline, and Molly pretend they don't notice the quiet. But that's impossible.

It's so quiet you can hear the crunch of each Dorito chip.

It's so quiet you can hear Charlotte L.'s lip gloss roll across the wooden table.

It's the most quiet a picnic has ever been.

Principal Finnery emerges from somewhere behind me. She's wearing strappy beige sandals with tiny heels that sink into the grass. But she's moving so fast and pumping her arms with such purpose that it looks like she's marching. "Would someone care to tell me what's going on here?" she says to Sophie and Amelia's table.

They look down at their laps. The only movement is Molly slowly licking orange Dorito dust off her fingers, one by one. Then Amelia raises her head and says softly, "Nothing."

"This doesn't look like nothing," says Principal Finnery. "This looks like the opposite of nothing."

"We're not doing anything," says Amelia. She elbows Sophie in the side.

"Yeah," mumbles Sophie.

"I'm not referring to what you're *doing*. I'm referring to what you're *wearing*. May I see those shirts?"

Amelia turns her body to face Principal Finnery. The crowd that has gathered shifts in one giant blob to see the shirts more clearly. The boy with his hands in his pockets, who is still standing a distance away, is the only one who doesn't move.

"*Stay. Away. From. Us.* Am I reading this correctly?" asks Principal Finnery. No one answers. "Where did you girls get these? And what in the world makes you think they're acceptable to wear to a school function?"

"Online," says Amelia. "And they don't say anything

bad. There aren't bad words or anything."

"Yes, I understand that, Amelia. But the spirit of the words is a different story. Please cover those up immediately, before this goes any further."

"But that's not fair," says Amelia. "We bought these with our own money. We're allowed to wear what we—"

Principal Finnery holds up one finger and Amelia gives a defeated sigh. The girls put their jackets and sweatshirts back on. But there's something in their faces, a tightness in their eyes and lips, that lets me know this is not the end.

It's only the beginning.

Dear Cove,

Sorry I haven't written in forever. School just started in NYC. I thought it was going to be terrible because when I went for a tour, the principal said I'm the only new kid in the entire grade. My favorite part of the tour was the swimming pool in the basement. I figured if things were terrible and everyone automatically hated me, I could hide underwater and pretend to be a mermaid all day long. Just like we used to in Eel Pond.

But it's actually not terrible. I got assigned this student mentor named Minnie (like the mouse). But no one calls her Minnie Mouse because she's super pretty and not the kind of girl you call Minnie Mouse. So forget I even said that!

Minnie's job was to show me around and introduce me to all her friends. So I didn't have to hide underwater. Minnie even saved a seat for me at her lunch table.

And I got a phone!!! My dads said they only let me get one because NYC is so big that it's for safety. That's why they won't let me buy a cool case. Not yet.

Please beg your mom for a phone so we can text. Emojis are so much faster than writing.

Love,
Nina

P.S. Here's a smiling emoji face because I'm so happy that people at school don't hate me. Hooray!

Dear Nina,

I wish I could go to your new school. It sounds so much better than here. I officially hate school without you. Sophie, Amelia, Molly, and Caroline wore shirts to the back-to-school picnic that say STAY AWAY FROM US in enormous letters. It's like the shirts are being mean for them so they don't even need to open their mouths anymore. Principal Finnery got super upset and made them cover up the shirts. But you could tell none of the teachers knew what to do.

I do have some good news. Or maybe it's more like medium news because it's just an idea. Remember that show I was telling you about called Create You? What if I applied to be on the show? I'd have to learn to sew before I can apply and I have no idea how I'm going to do that, but Jonah thinks I can draw just like the contestants on the show. If I get chosen, I could actually come to New York City and see you. What do you think? Should I try?

Or do you think Jonah was just being nice? I don't know, maybe it's just a dumb idea.

Please write back! I miss you!

Love,

Cove

P.S. This is a picture of the shirts. (The person whose head is on fire is Principal Finnery!)

Dear Cove,

OMG I hope you get on Create You! That would be awesome! You can do it! You're the best artist in our entire grade. Everyone knows that.

Did you ask your mom for a phone yet?

I have to go! I'm trying out for swim team! Wish me luck! I miss you!

Love,

Nina

P.S. Totally stinks about those shirts. I give that a sad emoji face.

12

I was right. The picnic was only the beginning. By the second week of school, a petition is going around. It says:

If you agree that according to the First Amendment of the United States of America we have a right to wear shirts that say whatever we want (not including swear words) sign here:

Everyone signs their names. Shocker. They don't sign because of the First Amendment. Everyone signs because Sophie and Amelia, and sometimes Caroline and Molly, walk around school and shove the petition in their faces. By the time Sophie gets to me at the end of the day, there are already ninety-seven names. I watch as Sophie flips through four pages on her clipboard, then uncaps the pen that is tied on with a rope of colorful strings knotted like a friendship bracelet.

"Here," she says.

I pretend to be confused.

"Um, Rover, the petition? You have to sign it. You must have heard. We're fighting for the right to freedom."

Freedom? They aren't fighting for freedom. They aren't fighting for anything except the right to wear mean shirts. I've watched Mom and her friends fight against all kinds of things. Big things like war, racism, and sexism. And smaller things like using lawn chemicals on the new eighteen-hole golf course in

West Tisbury. But no matter the cause, their protests work the same way. They make signs with big letters. They meet somewhere where lots of cars drive by. They chant: *"No More War!" "Smash the Glass Ceiling!" "Save Our Island!"* Even if the protestors are just going to support a friend, they all get really into it. One person starts chanting, then the others join in, and pretty soon they're all yelling and waving signs, and I end up sitting by the side of the road looking for four-leaf clovers.

If there's a petition, they don't decorate it with flowers and hearts and butterflies. They don't tell people to hurry up and sign because the bell's about to ring and they have to change for field hockey practice. They don't roll their eyes like Sophie when I ask, "What do you mean 'freedom'?"

"Like *freedom* freedom," says Sophie. "Don't you remember what Mr. Gabers taught us last year in social studies? The Founding Fathers and all that. We have rights."

"I don't know if that's what the Founding—"

"Oh, come on, Cove. Just sign. We're fighting for you, too. FYI."

"Me?" I almost look over my shoulder, that's how confused I am. "But I don't have one of those shirts."

"Obvs," says Sophie. "I'm pretty sure they don't come in dog sizes. But that's not the point. The point is you dress different. Like, different from everyone else. And no one tells you that you can't walk around dressed like a weirdo. We let you do it even though it's totally depressing to look at. So I'm just saying, you get it, right?"

Here's what I wish happens: I take her stupid clipboard and shove it in her stupid face. Or slam it on top of her stupid head.

Here's what actually happens: I nod, because if I don't move my head I'm worried Sophie will see the tears building in my eyes. I try to breathe, but it feels like my lungs are shrinking into tiny rocks. I reach for her pen even though my hands are shaking. Because I want to get away from Sophie as fast as I can, and that means signing the petition.

I hear words in my head. Words like *wrong*. And *mean*. And *bully*. But I don't say them out loud. Because it's suddenly easy to see myself exactly as Sophie sees me. As a weirdo. Someone who dresses differently because she's not allowed to wear neon shirts with black swooshes or interlocking Us. Someone who doesn't own a sweatshirt printed with the name of a vacation place because she's never been anywhere on vacation. Someone whose best friend moved far away and now has a super-pretty new friend named Minnie and a phone.

After I scrawl my name, I turn and walk away.

I try to look like I have somewhere to be.

Or someone to meet.

But I don't.

I pass posters for the robotics club and the a cappella

singing group. The improv group. All the construction paper is still bright and clean; the corners are crisp and sharp. A happy sparkling rainbow of afternoon activities just waiting for happy hands to write down happy names. Names like Grace and Alexandra. Kate. Isabelle. Chloe.

Not Cove.

Not Rover.

I promised Mom that today I would finally sign up for something to do after school. But I don't want to stay at school a minute longer than I have to. And besides, there's somewhere else where I can learn a lot more.

I keep walking.

I'm almost at the end of the hall that leads to the cafeteria when I see Molly sitting on the floor, her back against a metal locker, her pink Converse splayed out in front of her. "My dad keeps packing me stuff with nuts," she says, holding up a half-eaten pack of peanut butter crackers. "I got kicked out of the cafeteria. I'm not even supposed to be eating in the hallway, but these crackers are just so good. You want one?"

I almost sit down next to her. It would be so nice to sit and talk about something as normal as peanut butter crackers and their salty sweet deliciousness. But then I see what's next to Molly. A clipboard. It's turned over to face the floor, but it has string knotted like a friendship bracelet tied on to its metal clip.

And then I don't want to sit anywhere near her after all.

13

I take the number six bus straight from school to Sal's. After-school activities are usually two hours, so I figure Jonah and I can watch at least two more episodes of *Create You* before Mom starts to worry. I should start my homework on the bus. Instead, I look out the window. What Sophie said to me about the petition—the petition that I *signed*—bounces around my head like a trapped rubber ball. By the time I get to Sal's, it feels like the rubber ball will be stuck inside my head forever.

"Why so glum, chum?" asks Jonah. He turns the

page down on another thick book and slides a pen behind his ear. Jonah doesn't usually talk like that, all rhyme-y. But it doesn't take a genius to tell something's wrong.

"No reason," I say.

"Um, so not buying that," he says. "I'm thinking it's something really bad because you kinda look like this ratty old T-shirt. No offense."

Jonah holds up a faded blue T-shirt from a pile on the counter. It's full of tiny holes. The fabric is so thin that the light from the front window shines right through. It looks kind of beautiful, like a kaleidoscope Nina used to have, the kind that makes light seem like it's playing a game of tag. But that's not what Jonah means. He doesn't mean I look beautiful. He means I look pathetic. Sad. Worthless. The rubber ball in my head starts bouncing faster.

"Why does everyone think that if you just say 'no offense' it makes everything okay?" I ask. "Like, 'Cove, you're a total loser with no friends. *No offense.*'"

"Whoa there, partner," says Jonah, raising his hands in defense. "Rein it in."

But I don't want to stop.

"And why does everyone think they can say those kinds of things at all? Why do people think they can do stuff, like bark at you in the hallway or say they're fighting for your rights, when really they're just insulting you to your face? It's not like I go around asking you why you moved here and why you spend all day alone in a store underlining sentences in books and watching shows on your laptop. It's not like I say, 'Hey Jonah, why don't you try making some friends your own age? *No offense.*'"

The words come fast, before I can think them through. But even if I had thought them through, I still would have said them. Because I needed to know if they would make me feel better. I needed to know if being mean to someone else, someone you actually like, helps make everything else go away.

Turns out, it doesn't. Because I feel worse. Way worse.

"Are you done?" Jonah asks.

I nod.

"Well, that's a relief. Because that kind of stunk. *No offense.*"

"Sorry," I say. Even though I feel badly, I smile. I can tell by Jonah's tone of voice, by the way he flicks his head so that the spikes in his hair lean to the side, that he's not really truly mad.

"It's okay, Cove," says Jonah. "We all need to vent sometimes. Blow off a little steam. Any chance your particular steam blowing has something to do with what we were talking about last time?"

"You mean with *Create You?*" I ask.

"I mean with your long-lost BFF."

Jonah leans an elbow on the counter and balances his head in his hand. He wants me to start talking. But there's something I need to know first.

"Seriously," I say. "Why are you here?

"Ah," says Jonah. "Throwing it right back. In therapy, that's called deflecting. And yet, I will ignore your trickery and answer the question." He switches elbows and inhales. "I'm here because I had nowhere else I needed to be. I want to be a writer, so I applied to grad school thinking, 'No prob, I got this.' I quit my job, gave up my lease, the whole deal. But I didn't get in. I got wait-listed, which is pretty much worse than not getting in because it means I was super close, but just not quite good enough. a.k.a., I'm stuck in limbo. a.k.a., a unique form of waiting hell."

"Is that why you're always reading those thick books? Because you want to be a writer?"

"Congratulations, Sherlock Holmes. Consider the mystery solved."

"But why here?" I ask. "Why'd you come to Martha's Vineyard?"

Jonah pops the collar on his shirt. "What's so bad about here?"

"Are you deflecting?" I say, smiling.

He laughs. "Quite possibly. Now spill it. Tell me why you're so down in the dumps."

I tell Jonah the whole story. About Nina leaving, Sophie and Amelia at the Jaws Bridge, the picnic that's not really a picnic, the mean shirts, and the petition. I even tell him about the barking. I haven't had anyone to talk to about this stuff since Nina left. When I'm done, I feel so much better and so much worse. Better because I got it all out, like how my mom always says to blow out bad energy. But also worse, because now Jonah knows what the kids at school think about me.

"Damn," says Jonah when I finish. "I forgot how rough growing up can be. I know this is the part where I'm supposed to give you some insightful advice or whatever, but all I can think is that those shirts are an abominable abuse of fashion."

"Tell me about it," I say.

"There are only two people who can redeem the

world of fashion from such a horrendous atrocity."

"Benjamin Boyd and Martina Velez?"

"My thoughts exactly."

Jonah opens his laptop and pulls up *Create You*. He takes a package of multicolored Swedish Fish from his leather bag and tells me I can pick out all the red ones. But as I reach my hand in, Jonah pulls the bag away.

"You know you look nothing like a dog, right, Cove?" He says it more seriously than I've ever heard him say anything before. "Those girls, they're mean. They're just like mean girls everywhere, trying to bring down everyone around them to make themselves feel better. It's not about you; it's about them."

"I know," I say.

"Okay," he says. "Good. Just checking."

He hands me the bag of Swedish Fish. I pick a red one and stretch it as wide as I can before placing it in my mouth. I don't truly believe Jonah. I think those girls really do think I look like a dog. But as I cross my legs underneath me and the show begins, I feel better. The tall buildings of New York City flash across the screen. I don't look for Nina like I did before, but I do feel closer to her.

"Is everyone pumped for today's challenge?" asks Benjamin Boyd.

"Yes!" answers Jonah. "We're pumped!"

"Excellent," continues Benjamin Boyd. "Because today's challenge will require you to dig deep. Today you will be designing a symbol of appreciation. It can be any article of clothing designed for someone in your life, living or not, who you would like to thank for the impact they've had on your journey."

"Deep," says Jonah.

"Yeah," I say.

We watch as Carver sews a fancy dress for his grandmother to wear dancing, because she always told Carver to dance to his own beat. Mika sews a jacket for her mom, who makes her feel safe and warm. Paris sews a baggy pair of pants with wide leather suspenders for her older brother, because he helps her up whenever she falls down. Jonah and I laugh at that one.

Even as I focus on the details—the way Carver holds the scissors when he cuts an enormous piece of fabric, the way Mika drapes her mannequin, the way Paris hammers metal studs into leather—I think about what I would create. A string hangs down from the hood of my sweatshirt. Without looking away from the screen, my hands move the string in a familiar pattern. When the show breaks for a commercial, I realize I've tied a bowline knot. I imagine weaving a necktie of bowline knots. I would give it to Clark, to thank him for always making me feel special.

I remember something Nina said to Clark the afternoon we were learning the bowline. "The rope keeps slipping," she complained. "And it doesn't even make sense. Rabbits don't run around trees and through holes. This is stupid."

"Not everything has to make sense," responded Clark. "Sometimes you just have to feel your way through a challenge."

That made sense to me. Numbers, equations, puzzles, all the things that were so easy for Nina to figure out, didn't feel easy to me. They still don't. But guiding the singed end of a rope around itself and weaving it in just the right pattern, that I understood. I could picture the silly rabbit. I could feel the sturdy trunk of the tree. I could smell the dirt in the hole. Just like I can picture a necktie of bowline knots.

I can't make clothes out of singed rope and knots. But I do have ideas.

If I can learn to sew, maybe I really can get on *Create You*.

Maybe everything will be okay after all.

14

"Cove?" says Mom at dinner. "You there?"

"Yeah," I say, turning my head away from the window. "Just thinking."

"About what?"

"Learning to sew. I can't wait any longer."

"Have you decided on an after-school activity?" she asks. "I know you've been trying things, but you need to commit."

"Not yet. But I will. I promise."

Mom puts down her fork and knife. "I believe you, Cove. And you have to remember that sewing's not like soccer or ballet. We'll find lessons; it just might take some time."

"How much time?"

"However much it takes. Why? What's going on with you, Cove? Is there something you're not telling me?"

Yes! There's so much I'm not telling you! More than you could ever imagine! Instead of the truth, I shake my head.

"So it's not about the shirts?"

"What shirts?"

"The matching shirts that girls are wearing at school. Some of the moms were talking about them at yoga this morning. I couldn't believe it when I heard what was printed on the front. 'Stay away from us'? I mean, to think that anyone would want to broadcast such negativity. It's awful."

"What does that have to do with sewing?" I ask.

"Well, clearly kids at school are using clothing as a way to express themselves. I thought maybe that's why you were suddenly so interested in learning to sew. As a form of expression." Mom sounds so much like Benjamin Boyd and Martina Velez, the way they talk about fashion as a way to show the world who you are on the inside, that I don't know what to say. I feel like someone's taken a giant black Sharpie and drawn a line down the center of my body. One half wants to be the old me who told Mom everything. The other half wants to keep all my secrets tucked safe inside.

I go with the easier half. "Not everything is such a major deal, Mom," I say. "Sometimes people just want to learn something new. Can I be excused? I've got homework."

The teachers and staff still don't know what to do about the STAY AWAY FROM US shirts. Principal Finnery used to be really cheerful and give everyone high fives in the hallway. Now she walks around staring at clothes, like she's on the lookout for another student wearing one of the shirts. More kids have them now, even the ones who don't sit at Sophie and Amelia's lunch table. At morning assembly Principal Finnery starts her speech the same way she always does, but I can tell by her voice that she's not happy.

"Good morning, students and staff," she says.

"Good morning, Principal Finnery," everyone responds.

"As you all know, this is not a time of great pride for our school," says Principal Finnery. "The teachers and staff have been trying to find a way to address what's going on with the current, shall we say, *situation*. Until we come up with a permanent solution, we've decided that the entire school community needs a shift of focus. A *positive* shift of focus. So even though it's the beginning of the school year, we've decided that tomorrow we will be having a school-wide day of community service."

There are a few groans, but most people are

excited. Community service means leaving school. Leaving school means no classes. And no classes means no homework. The sound of creaking seats and voices spreads through the auditorium as everyone takes in the news.

"Settle down, settle down," says Principal Finnery. When no one listens, she puts two fingers to her mouth and raises her other hand in a peace sign, the way preschool teachers do when they're trying to quiet a class of four-year-olds. For a second I can pretend that I'm sitting on a colorful circle rug with the alphabet printed in primary colors, not a big middle school auditorium. I can pretend that everyone is excited because we're taking the class hermit crab out of its tank or someone's parents are bringing in cupcakes for a birthday snack.

For a second I can pretend that Nina is still here, sitting next to me.

When the noise doesn't stop, Principal Finnery

claps her hands into the microphone. The spell is broken.

"That is quite enough, students," she says. "Quite enough. Now, your homeroom teachers will be emailing the necessary information to your families. But before we part, I want to leave you with a reminder." She pauses and pushes her hair behind her ears. "Even though you will not be on school property, you will be representing our school. You will be in the community to help others and to learn from that experience. And I ask, along with my fellow teachers and staff, that you consider what that representation means and that you make an intelligent decision regarding your attire."

I'm sitting a few rows behind Sophie, Amelia, Caroline, and Molly. Amelia swishes her ponytail to her other shoulder. Sophie and Caroline look at each other. Molly looks down at her lap. Then someone behind me whispers, "Not a chance."

I turn. Sitting all alone is the boy I first saw at the

picnic, the one who was fiddling with something in his pockets. I've seen him in the hallway a few times and he always nods at me, like we've just finished some long conversation and come to an agreement, even though we haven't said a single word. He's wearing a faded black T-shirt, like always. His arms are resting on the backs of the seats next to him. He whispers, "Never. Gonna. Happen."

"What?" I whisper back, even though I know what he's talking about. Something about him, maybe the way he's leaning back in his seat, makes me think that if I don't keep him talking, I'll blink and he'll be gone. Like he's someone I'm imagining. Like Nina.

"Come on," he says. "I can tell you know."

Before I can answer, the assembly is over. Backpack buckles bang against armrests, the floor vibrates with shuffling feet. I reach down to get my own backpack. When I look back up, he's already walking away.

I can tell you know.

Five words.

Not even particularly nice words.

But they are some of the nicest words anyone has said to me at school in a long time.

"Wait up," I call.

He shrugs, like he could easily walk out the door and keep going until he hits the ocean, or stand right there waiting until the end of the day. He looks like nothing in the world could ever bother him. Like anything bad would roll off his shoulders and land on the tiled floor by his boots.

"Why did you say that?" I ask.

"Say what?"

"I can tell you know."

"Well, don't you know?"

"I do. But I still want to know why you said it."

He shrugs again. "I had something to say and you looked like the kind of person to say it to."

We are standing outside the doors to the

auditorium. Everyone's moving in different directions, heading toward different classrooms at the ends of different hallways. I get bumped by a random elbow. But the boy doesn't seem to mind the jostling crowd. It's like his boots are glued to the ground.

"I'm Jack, by the way."

"Cove."

"Cool," he says. "See you around."

He turns to walk away, and I notice a group of chains that hang from a loop on the waist of his jeans to his front pocket. They're silver, shiny and uneven, but I can't tell what they're made of. They remind me of something Paris would add to one of her *Create You* designs for texture. "Wait," I say, nodding toward the chain. "What's that?"

"One of my creations," says Jack. He lifts the chains. They're attached at both ends, so they don't move that much. But now I can tell that they're some combination of paper clips and metal tabs, the kind that come from a can of soda.

"You made that?" I ask.

"Yup."

"How?"

"You ever heard of dumpster diving?" asks Jack.

"No," I say.

"Well, then, you're missing out."

15

The next morning four school buses are parked outside of school. On the side of each bus is a colored piece of paper—green, blue, purple, and red. I have no idea what the colors mean until I get to homeroom, where Mr. Turner passes out sealed envelopes with our names written on the front. "Inside each envelope is a color," he explains. "When it's time to leave, you will get on the bus that matches your color."

"This is totally sketchy," says Sophie as she waves her envelope in the air. "You're not going to, like, kidnap us or anything, are you?"

"No, Sophie," says Mr. Turner. "We're not going to, *like*, kidnap you." Mr. Turner doesn't usually talk this way. I think it's because Sophie's wearing her STAY AWAY FROM US shirt and there's not a thing Mr. Turner can do about it.

"I agree with Sophie," says Amelia. "There's a total creep factor happening here."

"You know we live on an island, right?" says Gavin. "It's not like we can go very far."

"Duh," says Amelia. "But that doesn't mean this whole mystery color thing isn't sketchy."

"What's sketchy is your logic," says Gavin.

"Enough!" says Mr. Turner, banging a flat hand on his desk. "Enough from all of you. Today is about community building. It's not about where you're going or who you're going with. We're coming together to do some good. We will learn to— "

Mr. Turner stops talking mid-sentence. I feel badly for him, but only just a little. I don't know why the teachers think this day is going to help. Getting on a bus and leaving school isn't going to change who anyone is or how they act. If anything, it's going to make everyone act more like who they really are.

The popular girls will squeeze together in a single row of seats. With their power condensed and the barriers of the seat protecting them, they'll act like no one can hear the mean things they whisper. Only that's not true at all. Because as soon as the bus starts moving, they'll start talking louder and louder until everyone around them can hear. That's the whole point. The boys in the back will lean over their seats and yell out the windows. And me, I'll sit somewhere near the middle, pretending that I belong where I am, even though I have no idea where I belong at all.

I get the color blue, which is the last bus in the line. Even though I'm not sure it's the right decision, I board the bus as soon as I can. I think about waiting and getting on last, because then I wouldn't have to choose where to sit. Or at least, I wouldn't have so many choices. But it's just as bad to stand outside the bus acting like you're waiting for someone as it is to be inside the bus pretending someone is looking for you.

I pick a seat by the window, so I can see what buses other kids are getting on. Sophie's holding a red piece of paper and Amelia's holding a green piece of paper. They hug good-bye and wipe fake tears from their eyes. Molly has a blue piece of paper, but she doesn't hug anyone. Then Jack walks out of school. After morning assembly yesterday I didn't see him at all, even though I kept looking. As the day went on, I thought of more and more questions. Like how'd he make that chain? What is dumpster diving? Where did he come from? And why did he choose to talk to me?

Jack's wearing his same black T-shirt. Chains are hanging from his pocket.

He's holding a blue piece of paper. He walks straight onto my bus.

"Taken?" he asks, looking at the empty seat next to me.

I shake my head.

"Dope," he says, and plops down.

The bus pulls out of the school parking lot with a loud screech. As we turn a corner, I have to hold on to the seat in front of me with both hands so that I don't lean into Jack. But I do glance down to get a better look at the chains attached to his jeans. They seem a little bigger today, like there's one more strand.

"Did you add more?" I say.

"Oh, yeah," he says. "I had a great dive yesterday. Look, I found this." He points to a blue tab in the center of the new strand. It's attached to the other tabs by an unwound paper clip on one end and a group of staples on the other end. "You can only get the blue ones from certain beer cans. Some PBRs. Vintage

Budweisers. I guess that's how the people roll on this island, because I found a bunch of these down by the harbor."

"So you mean you actually dive into dumpsters? Like trash dumpsters?" I sniff the air between us. I can't help it; just talking about diving into a trash dumpster makes me think that Jack should smell really bad. But he doesn't. I don't smell anything other than the normal school bus smell of rotting fruit and plastic.

Jack smiles. "I mean, you don't really dive. Not like headfirst. More like you scrounge. You keep your eyes open. Always looking. And if that means sticking your hand into a few trash cans, then yeah. That's what you do."

"How'd you learn to do it?" I ask.

Jack adjusts the chain against his pocket. "It's not the kind of thing you have to learn. It's not like they have dumpster-diving classes after school. You just start doing it. Like when I was little, I'd have to hang around my mom's office for hours. I got bored and I just started taking things, mostly from the supply closet, but sometimes from trash cans. Paper clips, pen caps, tape—the kind of stuff that no one notices. I started to string them together. Then it just grew from there. It's insane what people throw away. I've lived all over the world and it's always the same deal. Trash, trash, trash. No wonder the planet is literally melting. Why, you want to give it a try someday?"

"Yeah," I say. "I kinda do. There's this show I like called *Create You* where the contestants have to make clothes. There's a girl named Paris who always adds metal to her designs. That's totally the kind of thing she would do on the show."

"Dumpster dive? For real? I've got to check that out. What channel is it on?"

"Oh," I say. "Um, I don't know. I watch it with a friend while we work at this store called Sal's. My friend brings his laptop. But I don't think they would actually dumpster dive on the show. I don't know why I said that." My cheeks get red. I shift in the seat. I need to change the subject before Jack catches on that my *friend* is a grown-up and that neither of us actually *work* when I'm at Sal's. "I want to be a fashion designer when I'm older, so . . ."

The words come out of my mouth as easily as if I'd said my name is Cove and I live on Martha's Vineyard. But I'm not sure the words are even true. I mean, I want to get on *Create You*. I need to get on *Create You*. But what I want to be when I'm older, I have no idea.

I look down at the dirty bus floor that is marked with footprints and scraps of paper. I can't imagine what Jack is thinking. Jack who has lived all over the world. Jack who makes cool metal chains out of trash and loops them onto his jeans. Jack who says, "Yeah, I could see you being that. Maybe I could watch the show with you and your friend someday."

16

The bus ride is short because it turns out we are only going a few blocks away, to the Vineyard Senior Center. The first thing I notice when we walk inside is the wallpaper. It has huge roses with lots of twisting green vines creeping their way over a creamy background. The second thing I notice is how still it is. The room is full of people, but they're not moving. Most are sitting on couches and chairs, but even the ones who are standing are still. They lean on walkers or have their hands clasped in front of their bodies. It makes me feel still, too. I'm not the only one.

"Go ahead, guys," says Ms. Ratowski, our art teacher and one of the chaperones. "Introduce yourselves. Meet the residents. Ask them about their hobbies and what they like to do. Remember, we're here to brighten their day. Provide companionship."

No one moves. It's a face-off, young versus old. Then someone behind me pushes forward. Jack. He walks up to a man sitting on a bench in front of a piano. "Know any new stuff?" says Jack. The old man laughs, and they flip through the pages of a music book that is resting against a stand.

It's not like Jack starts an avalanche or anything. But slowly some of our group walks over to some of their group. Molly comes up beside me and asks, "Want to go together?" I know she's wearing her shirt because I saw it this morning. But she's covered it up with a teal sweatshirt even though it's much warmer inside the Vineyard Senior Center than it is inside school.

My first thought is to say no. Molly doesn't really want to be my friend. She doesn't need to be. She's got all her mean-shirt-wearing besties who talked super loudly in homeroom about the movie they're going to see this weekend. But then I remember the thumbtack and the nurse. The peanut butter crackers. I think about how fun it was to talk to Jack on the bus. But mostly I think about Nina and what it felt like to have a friend by my side. "Okay," I say.

"Cool!" she says. "Which one? You pick."

I look around the room, unsure of who to choose. There's an old woman knitting with purple yarn. She looks pretty nice. There's a man in a wheelchair coughing into a plaid handkerchief. Then I see a woman walking down the hall. She's wearing a gray cardigan with wood buttons. Her hair is in a neat bun. I recognize her from Sal's. "How about her?" I say to Molly.

We follow the old woman down the hall and watch

as she turns into a room with 2F printed next to the open door. There's a neatly made bed with floral pillowcases. A wooden dresser whose top is covered in white lace and photographs in mismatched frames. In one corner of the room is a rocking chair with a scratchy-looking blanket folded over the back. And in another corner, on a desk, is a sewing machine. It's small and black, not like the huge white ones they use on *Create You*. But I can see thread running from the top of the machine into the needle and a foot pedal on the floor. I take a step forward.

"May I help you?" the old woman asks.

I know it doesn't make any sense, but her voice surprises me. Not the way it sounds, but that she even has one. It's like the sewing machine casts some spell on me. I can't look away from it.

"Is that a sewing machine?" I ask.

"Yes," she says.

"Does it work?"

"Indeed."

"Can you show me how?"

"Well, I do believe introductions may be in order first."

Molly nudges me and I look away from the sewing machine. "Oh," I say. "I'm Cove. Sorry. I just really want to learn how to sew and you actually have a sewing machine."

Molly waves one hand. "And I'm Molly."

"Well, Cove-who-really-wants-to-learn-how-to-sew and Molly, I'm Anna. It's a pleasure to meet you both. Why don't you come in." She motions for us to enter the room. I walk straight to the desk.

"Can I touch it?" I ask, reaching out.

"Assuming it no longer bites."

I pull my hand back. Molly laughs. "She's joking, Cove."

"Right," I say, shaking my head. I reach my hand out again, toward the curve of the machine's top. But just as I'm about to make contact, there's a loud clap. I jolt back.

"My apologies," says Anna, laughing. "I simply could not resist."

Molly puts her arm over her mouth to quiet her giggles, but it doesn't take long for full-on laughter to break through. Within seconds Molly's bent over laughing and I'm shaking my head laughing and Anna's leaning on the edge of the wooden dresser laughing. When we finally stop, I wipe my eyes and take a deep breath. I haven't laughed that much since before Nina left. Long enough ago that I forgot how good it feels.

"It was so cool," I tell Mom at dinner that night. "The sewing machine made this thumping noise as the needle went in and out of the fabric. And the harder you push on the foot peddle, the faster the needle moves. I guess that makes it kind of like driving a car, right?"

Mom brings her mug of green tea to her lips, but she doesn't take a sip. And she doesn't answer.

"What?" I ask.

"Nothing." But it's not nothing. Her eyes squint a little and her lips curl up behind the rim of the mug, giving her a half-happy, half-sad look that makes me feel embarrassed even though I didn't do anything embarrassing.

"Mom," I say. "Tell me."

"It's just, there are moments when you can see someone's spirit dance. And this is one of those moments. Just now, when you were talking about learning to sew, I saw your spirit dance. And it made me realize how long it's been since I've seen you like this. Probably since Nina moved away. And I'm grateful. I'm grateful to the universe for giving you this day."

I reach out to touch the top edge of the candle where it's soft and warm. The hot wax flows onto my fingertip. "I didn't know . . . I didn't know if you would think that."

"Cove, why?"

Because you don't know, I think. *You don't know the reason why I'm so happy. It has nothing to do with spirits or dancing or the universe. It has to do with finding a way to see Nina again. With applying to* Create You. *With leaving the island.*

But instead I say, "Because I haven't signed up for anything after school yet."

"True," says Mom. "But it sounds like fate had a hand in this. And fate tends to overlook practical things like sign-up sheets. Now, tell me more about this Anna."

I smile. "Well, she knows a ton about fashion. She used to be a seamstress. She made clothes for Coco Chanel in Paris. She said the women who worked at Coco Chanel had to wear white gloves when they touched the clothes so that the oil from their fingers didn't hurt the fabric. And that the clothes were so amazing and expensive that customers would practically sell their own children to be able to buy them."

Mom huffs. "Well, I'm sure that's not all true. Anna was probably trying to make a point about the addictive quality of luxury consumer goods, which is something you already know."

"Right," I say, picking the hardened wax off my fingertip. "I already know."

Mom puts her hand over mine so that I can't pick anymore. "Hey, Cove," she says. "Since we're sharing good news, I've got something to tell you."

"Okay," I say.

"You remember Sean, right? From the beach in Menemsha?"

I nod.

"Well, we've been hanging out some more. It's not a big deal, but I like him. He makes me feel, I don't know, more whole. I want us all to spend some time together so you two can get to know each other."

I pull my hand out from under hers. I look out the window.

"Cove, sweetie. Did you hear me?"

"Yeah," I say. "I heard you. It's fine. I don't care."

"Clearly, you do."

"No, Mom. I don't."

"Okay, Cove. Let the idea rest inside you. It's a lot to take in. Give yourself time."

"But I thought you said it's not a big deal?"

It's back. That same feeling of being split in half, like someone's drawn a line down the middle of my body with black Sharpie. Half of me wants to be happy for Mom, but the other half feels angry. And jealous.

No wonder Mom thinks the universe is so giving.

It gives people right to her, while it takes my best friend away from me.

Dear Nina,

Do you remember when we were little and we wanted everything to be fair? Like when we got a bag of candy, the first thing we'd do is divide it up by color and shape. We never took a single bite until our piles were perfectly even. Remember the gummy worms that were impossible to break? No matter how hard we pulled they would stretch and stretch but never rip in equal halves. That's how I feel now. Like I'm stuck with the small half of a stretched-out gummy worm and things are never going to be fair again. Mom officially has a new boyfriend and you're still gone. She's all happy and I'm all alone.

The only good thing is that I found someone to teach me how to sew. We had this community service day today because the teachers thought it would magically fix everything with the STAY AWAY FROM US shirts. It didn't fix anything (shocker), but we did go to this place where older people live and I met this really nice lady. Her name is

Anna and she said she can teach me how to sew. She used to work for a world-famous fashion designer named Coco Chanel. Have you ever heard of her?

If Anna teaches me to sew then maybe, maybe, maybe I'll actually get on Create You. Then something good will happen. But until then, I don't know what I'm going to do.

I miss you. Write back.

Love,
Cove

P.S. Here's a picture of a broken gummy worm.

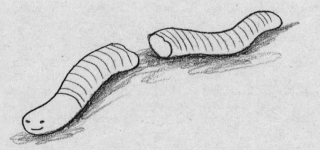

Dear Nina,

Did you get my letter? The one about gummy worms and learning to sew? I sent it last week. Please write back!

Love,
Cove

P.S. Here's a picture of my fingers. That's blood squirting everywhere because I keep pricking myself with sewing needles! Sewing is much harder (and bloodier) than it looks.

Dear Cove,

Sorry it's taken me so long to write back. I have so much homework and swim team and sometimes we forget to check the mail until the weekend. I totally know who Coco Chanel is. There's a Chanel store on Madison Avenue. That's the street that has all the super-fancy and expensive stores. I think Minnie's mom has a bunch of bags from Chanel because they have a CC logo on them in gold. I'll check next time I go to her apartment. Her mom's closet is so big that sometimes we just hang out in there looking at all her things.

Minnie's closet isn't as big as her mom's, but she still has so many clothes. She's letting me borrow a dress to wear to Papa's gallery show. Did I tell you about that? It's in a few weeks. They're filling the entire gallery with just his paintings. The opening party is late at night, and I get to miss school the next day!!

I wish you had a phone because then I could text you a picture of my dress. Or actually, Minnie's dress. But I wish it was mine! It's soooo pretty! I love it!

Love,

Nina

17

The number six bus goes from school to the Vineyard Senior Center. I'm walking out of school toward the bus stop when I hear someone call my name. "Cove! Yo, wait up!"

It's Jack. He's running and his backpack bounces up and down on his shoulders, making him look like a little kid. Or maybe not a little kid exactly. He's wearing too much black and his dumpster-diving chains. Maybe it's that the backpack bouncing makes him look lighter. Less serious than he usually does.

"Where you going?" he asks.

"Home," I lie.

"So you're taking the long way around the island? You must really love buses."

It takes me a bit to realize that Jack knows I live up island, in Chilmark, and the bus I'm waiting for is going down island, toward Edgartown. Which means that to get to my house going this direction I would be taking a bus around almost the entire island. Here's the thing: I know where Jack lives, too. I heard some kids say that Jack's mom is this super-famous architect and that she travels around the world designing beach houses for mega rich people. I know they're living on Davis Lane because Amelia's mom helped them find the house, and Amelia told everyone that Jack's mom drives a car with doors that open like wings, straight up. That's mostly what they talked about, the car with wings.

But I had no idea Jack knew anything about me. What else does he know?

Does he know that I've never left this island? Not once.

Has he heard girls bark at me?

What does he think if he did?

The sun is shining in my eyes so it gives me an excuse to look down at the sidewalk. "I'm stopping somewhere first," I say.

"The old people's home?"

"How did you know?" Seriously, how does he know all this? No one from school knows that I've been going to see Anna. The only person I told was Jonah. I almost told Molly. But then I thought about how Molly wore the STAY AWAY FROM US shirt underneath her teal sweatshirt on the day we met Anna and I changed my mind.

"You're not the only one with friends in lonely places," says Jack.

I shake my head, confused.

"It's a song. About lonely places. Or something

like that. Walt, that guy at the piano, said he would teach me some of his favorite songs. So I went over there once. Walt said this girl my age has been coming by, and I knew right away he was talking about you."

"How?" I ask. But then I wish I could take the question back. There are too many answers that will make me feel terrible.

The girl who dresses in all those plain clothes.

The girl who looks sad.

The girl who's always alone.

Jack shrugs and says, "Just did."

The bus pulls up with a loud mechanical groan. Jack sits on the seat next to me and we ride the whole way together.

"Guide, don't pull," says Anna as my fingers spread across a piece of navy silk. The fabric is slippery and it bunches underneath the sewing machine's presser foot, creating tiny ripples along the seam.

"Guide, don't pull," I repeat to myself. I try to lift my hands from the fabric so that I'm not pressing as hard. But I accidentally push down on the foot pedal, causing the needle to speed up and the fabric to bunch even more. "I can't do it," I say. "It's too slippery."

"You *can* do it, Cove. You just need to listen to the fabric under your fingers." Anna moves her fingers like she's mimicking a wave. Her hands are thin, with brown spots and raised veins. The first time we sewed together, I had a hard time looking at them. I've seen lots of old people's faces, but I've never noticed their hands. Anna's hands made me feel sad, like something bad had happened to them. But I don't think that anymore. I've seen what Anna's hands can do. When Anna sits at the sewing machine, the fabric is under her command.

"Can't we just do something else?" I ask. "Like maybe design something?"

"We cannot."

"But I don't even like this fabric. It's too shiny."

"It's not a matter of what you like. It's a matter of what you learn. You learn, then you like."

Anna's always saying things like this, things that make it hard to answer back. What am I supposed to say? That I'm tired of learning? That I'm tired of sewing practice seam after practice seam on scraps of fabric? That I just want to see Nina again? Even though I don't say these things, Anna must see the words in my eyes. "Stretch," she says.

I push back from the sewing machine and reach my hands over my head. I've been looking at tiny stitches for so long that I have to blink to bring the rest of the room into focus. The floral pillowcases on her bed. The white lace cloth on the dresser. The black-and-white photographs.

"Is this your family?" I ask, looking at the pictures. There are two girls wearing white dresses, women in black dresses trimmed in lace, and tall men with beards and round hats.

"Yes," she says. She nods at the picture of the two girls. "That is me and my sister. In France. She died a very long time ago." Anna stares at the picture, and I worry she's going to keep talking almost as much as I worry that she's going to stop. "Do you know why sewing brings me such joy, Cove?"

I don't answer. There's something in the air, a thickness, that makes me not want to speak.

"Because you start with nothing. You spread your materials on your worktable and they're flat and lifeless. Then you start to cut and stitch. You stitch and you stitch and those stitches grow. Something forms. Like a gown. A gown so beautiful that it gets put in the window of the atelier. Women stop on the street and stare. They imagine who they would be in that dress. Then one day, a woman tries it on. A woman who's going through a difficult time, perhaps. She steps into the gown and feels the silk lining against her skin, the way the sleeve kisses her wrist. And it changes her, the dress. When she puts it on, she becomes someone else. A woman with less troubles, or sometimes more. But always, she is changed."

Yes! I want to say. *I understand! I've seen how the shirts at school have changed the way people walk, talk, act.* I almost tell Anna why I'm really here. But she doesn't blink, doesn't move her eyes from the window. She's talking about dresses, but her face makes it clear that she's thinking of something way bigger.

I find Jack in the lobby. He looks like he's having a much better time. There are empty Jell-O containers stacked on the side of the piano like blocks. He and Walt are playing drums on the bench with plastic spoons.

"Grab a spoon," says Jack when he sees me. "We're rocking out."

"No, thanks," I say. "I'm going to head home." I start to walk away.

"Hey, wait up," calls Jack. "I'll come with you." Jack gives Walt a high five. I just left Anna's room with a pathetic wave.

"Dude, what happened to you in there?" asks Jack when we get outside. "You look . . . I don't know . . . bummed."

"Nothing," I say, which is actually true. Nothing happened. I mean, I sewed. I watched the needle rise and fall, over and over. But I didn't make anything.

"Well," says Jack. "Want to do something?"

I shake my head. I'm not in the mood to do anything except go home.

"Trust me," says Jack. "You want to do *this*."

Turns out dumpster diving is the perfect way to feel better. Jack really wants to find some more blue tabs, the kind that come from beer cans he thinks fishermen like to drink. So we take the bus down to the docks in Menemsha and start looking behind Larsen's Fish

Market. It smells more like raw fish than garbage. They're similar smells, but also different. Raw fish smells salty, like the ocean. And there aren't any actual dumpsters, which helps. Just a few half-full trash cans behind Larsen's and a few more next door at the Texaco gas station. The trash cans are dark green, covered with old gum and whatever dried liquid leaves a brownish, grayish, gooey stream behind. Jack walks up to the first trash can and stares it down.

"All right, my friend," says Jack. "It's just you and me. We're all alone in this world. Let's see what you've got."

I laugh and give it a try. "You, too," I say to the other trash can. "Bring it on."

"Trash talk. Nice. You're a natural."

"I don't know. I'm not actually sure I can do it." I stare into the trash can. There are mussel and oyster shells. Styrofoam cups with the remains of clam chowder. Crumbs of crackers mixed with orange soda.

Gum wrappers, plastic forks, and a faded newspaper with a picture of a child staring up at me with big eyes. Just an hour before I was sitting in Anna's quiet room with her basket of fabric scraps on my lap. The same fabric scraps that bunched in my fingers and made the sewing machine needle jam with tangled thread. I think about how frustrated that made me. How angry.

I close my eyes and reach in.

A whole new smell rises up. It's nothing like raw fish. It's nothing like salt water.

Something catches in my throat. Like I'm going to puke.

I close my eyes.

But then Jack is next to me.

"Cove, look," he says. "Right there."

There's a beer can with a shiny blue tab. I grab it as carefully as I can, trying not to touch anything that I don't have to.

"See," says Jack. "I knew you were a natural."

The beer can is surprisingly clean, not a single dent. "You can have it," I say.

"No way, finders keepers. It's all yours."

I rock the tab back and forth until it pops off with a metallic clink. I put it in my pocket and Jack searches for more.

In my pocket the tab feels much bigger than it actually is. I run my finger over its metal surface, like I need to keep checking that it's still there. I realize that's what Jack must have been doing on the day of the back-to-school picnic. That's why he kept taking his hands in and out of the pockets of his jeans.

I smile. Nina and I used to talk about everything. And when we weren't talking, we'd look at each other to make sure that the other person understood what neither of us was saying out loud.

Jack and I aren't like that. We don't talk all that much. Sometimes on the bus we just stare out the window. And we definitely don't look at each other the way Nina and I used to. But with this blue tab in my pocket, I understand Jack a little better.

And maybe that means he understands me, too.

Even though that's not the same thing as having your best friend around, it's better than nothing. It's something. Even if that something came from a trash can covered in slime.

October

18

"It's the most wonderful time of the year," sings our art teacher, Ms. Ratowski, as she dances around the room in her black clogs and paint-splattered smock. She twirls toward the back of the room where Jack is sitting at the last table because he slipped in the door just as the bell rang. Then Ms. Ratowski twirls back to the front, passing Sophie and Amelia and pretending to sprinkle fairy dust on their heads. "La, la, la, la. It's the most wonderful time of the year!"

Everyone knows Ms. Ratowski's singing a Christmas song. Only it's not close to Christmas. It's

October. The thing about Ms. Ratowski is she doesn't always make sense. Like she knows a ton of languages and she throws foreign words into sentences whenever she can. Some kids think she's wacky, but I think she does it on purpose because she likes to be different.

"Does anyone know why October is the most wonderful time of the year?" Ms. Ratowski does the singing voice again, this time in a really high pitch.

"Because our teacher's lost it?" asks Hunter Gilford. It's not the kind of thing you can say to most teachers, especially if you're Hunter, but Ms. Ratowski smiles.

"*Nein*," she says. "Strike one."

"Because Stop and Shop just got their monster bags of Halloween candy?" asks Gavin. "Watch out aisle six! I'm coming in!"

"Strike *dos*. But closer."

It must have something to do with Halloween. Pumpkins? Costumes? I'm not sure. Then I think of the straw tepee at Morning Glory Farm. In the beginning of October, the people at Morning Glory make a tepee out of straw and put it in the middle of the farm's pumpkin patch. Nina and I love to sit in the tepee. Or we used to, before she left. The straw would prick our arms and legs, but it felt so safe inside. So secret. So I blurt out, "The tepee at Morning Glory?"

I immediately realize my mistake. The sound of laughter floats in the air. I'm not exactly sure who's laughing, because it's not the kind of laughter that happens when something's funny. It's not the kind where some people chuckle, and other people giggle, and other people snort through their nose and wipe tears from their eyes. It's the other kind. The kind that's quieter and blends together because the thing that happened is not funny, it's embarrassing. Someone from the side of the room whispers, "Does anyone still play in that thing?"

"I guess Cove does," says Amelia. She's wearing her STAY AWAY FROM US T-shirt underneath an unzipped blue hoodie. Some of the letters are covered by the sides of the hoodie, but that doesn't matter. Everyone in school knows what it spells.

My face gets hot. I run my fingers over the ridges in the table, the straight-edged lines from years of X-Acto knives and Scotch tape. I pick at the edge of a really old piece of tape, but it doesn't budge.

Ms. Ratowski must have heard Amelia, because she doesn't even say "Strike three." Instead she claps her hands, stands right next to Amelia, and announces: "Because it's scarecrow-making time! Time to get this island in the Halloween spirit, my *petits artistes!*"

Argh. I can't believe I didn't think of that. The Scarecrow Stroll! Every year before Halloween, schools and businesses dress scarecrows in different themes. The scarecrows line the main streets of the towns, all silly and droopy-looking, propped up against lamp posts and store doors. On the afternoon of the Scarecrow Stroll, the shops hand out candy and hot apple cider, or sometimes even caramel apples. It's one of my favorite afternoons of the year.

"Let's do a zombie scarecrow," says Hunter.

"A poop emoji scarecrow," says Gavin.

"A zombie scarecrow holding a phone with a poop emoji on the screen," says Hunter.

"*Tranquilo, tranquilo,*" says Ms. Ratowski, holding up her hands for everyone to stop talking. "We're doing things a little differently this year. Normally each art class constructs one scarecrow. As a group. But this year, given the . . ." She pauses and puts the tip of a paintbrush to her lips. "Shall we say, in plain English, *the spirit of the school,* every student will design an individual mini-scarecrow that represents their best self. Their ultimate future self. Then the teachers and staff will pick one scarecrow design to display on the street to represent our school. *Bien?*"

Everyone nods, because that's what you do when teachers ask those kind of questions.

Even if you worry that your best self might have gotten left behind in the past.

"What's an atelier?" I ask Jonah that afternoon as I take a seam ripper to a pair of torn blue jeans. I've been sewing with Anna a lot, but last week she said she had to go off island today for a doctor's appointment. "A few routine medical examinations" was all she would tell me. So I go to Sal's instead. And it's such a nice change. I mean, I'm grateful to Anna for teaching me to sew on her sewing machine, but she's still so concerned with how straight and even my stitches are that I spend just as much time fixing my work as I do constructing it. At the rate Anna and I are going, I'm never going to sew well enough to apply to *Create You*.

Although, it's not all Anna's fault. I'm the one who hasn't told her about *Create You*. It's not that Anna wouldn't understand the show. She doesn't have a TV or a smartphone, but neither do I and I still get it.

It's more that I know how much sewing means to her. There's a look that comes over Anna's face when the needle is going straight and the fabric is cooperating. It reminds me of Mom when she's meditating. Or Nina when she's about to snap in the final pieces of a one-thousand-piece puzzle. You just know that something important is happening to the other person, even if it doesn't seem important to you. It floats in the air like a flashing sign, warning you not to interrupt.

I'm worried that if I tell Anna the real reason I want to learn to sew, she'll be disappointed. Maybe so disappointed that she'll stop teaching me.

But Jonah gets it, of course. He's been saving the clothes that are too beat-up to sell in a special pile. First he cuts the clothes into pieces, then he spreads the pieces on the counter and tells me to close my eyes. When I open my eyes, he's jumbled them up. I have to put the pieces back together like one of Nina's puzzles. It's hard, but Jonah says I need to understand how shapes form real clothes if I want to have a shot at designing something good enough to get me on *Create You.*

"An ahh-tell-yay," says Jonah, correcting my pronunciation and sounding exactly like Anna. "It's a workroom. An old-fashioned design studio. Picture lots of serious women in white coats sewing five hundred thousand tiny pearl beads onto the world's most fabulous ball gown."

"Five hundred thousand?" I can't even imagine what five hundred thousand pearl beads would look like. And I definitely can't imagine how long it would take to sew them onto a gown.

"Possible exaggeration," says Jonah. "My point is, the work they do in those places is incredible. Super labor-intensive. Why do you ask?"

I shrug. "It's just a word Anna used. I didn't know what it meant. Do you think that's what Anna did for Coco Chanel? Sewed pearls onto dresses all day?"

"Probably," says Jonah, leaning back against the counter. "I read a book about Coco Chanel once. Apparently she was absolutely fabulous and absolutely evil, all at the same time."

"But she's so famous. How could she be evil?"

"Trust me, the two can go hand in hand."

Jonah pretends like his two hands are fighting with each other. I'm laughing, so I don't notice the door to Sal's open. But Jonah does and he stands up straight. "Welcome to Salvatore's," he says in a way that makes the words sound like a grand announcement. I turn to the door. It's Jack. Jack who I lied to about working at Sal's with a friend. I start to clear the cut-up pieces of fabric from the table, trying to look busy. I haven't told Jonah about Jack because I knew that whatever I said, it was going to come out wrong.

There's this new boy at school, and we sit together on the bus sometimes. One time we went dumpster diving.

He's different. I like him.

But not like that.

We're just friends.

Really.

"Jack," I say nervously. "What are you doing here?"

"I don't know," says Jack. "Just thought you might be working today."

"You two know each other?" asks Jonah.

"From school," I say. I watch Jonah to see if he's going to say anything about Jack's work comment. Or make a big deal about a boy from school coming to visit me. But he doesn't. Not at all.

"Nice," says Jonah. "Does that mean it's cool to put on some *Create You?*"

"Yes," I say. "Definitely cool."

19

The weather turns crisp and cool. Lockers become crowded as coats and backpacks compete for space. Jack doesn't come with me to the Vineyard Senior Center for the entire week, and I don't know why. By Friday I stand at the bus stop and try not to look like I'm waiting for him. But I can't stop glancing toward the front doors of school, hoping that Jack will open them and walk in my direction. I've brought my blue tab in case he wants to go dumpster diving again. I take it out of my pocket and hold it in my hand, the metal warming in my tight grip.

What could I have done to make Jack stop hanging out with me? That afternoon at Sal's was a regular Swedish Fish-eating, *Create You*-watching afternoon. Jonah didn't give away that I don't work there or say anything about the idea of applying to the show. He just sat back and let me and Jack do most of the talking. At first we talked about the contestants. But then we talked about school things, like the zombie poop emoji scarecrow and what that would look like if it got drenched in rain. "You two are beyond disgusting," Jonah said as he shivered and covered his ears. Jack and I laughed so hard that we couldn't even hear what Benjamin Boyd and Martina Velez were saying.

When the bus pulls up, I'm smiling at the thought of Jonah's appalled face. I take a seat toward the front, by the window. I sit up on my knees to look out once more for Jack.

"Waiting for someone?" asks the driver. He's watching me through the rearview mirror.

I shake my head. I put my backpack next to me. It slides off the curved plastic seat as the bus pulls into the road.

"Ah, Cove," says Anna when I knock on her door. "I'm all ready for you. Come in." The wooden rocking chair that is usually in the corner is pushed closer to the dresser. In its place is a mannequin on a pole.

I walk over to the mannequin and run my hand down its side. It's made of soft cream fabric that feels like the really old T-shirts that get donated to Sal's. The mannequin curves in at the waist and back out at the hips, with two small breasts that look like tennis balls cut in half. The mannequin would probably be a two in Nina's book, maybe a three.

"I call her Adela," says Anna.

"She has a name?"

"Of course. Whenever you are designing, you must have a muse. An inspiration. An image in your mind of the woman who will wear your clothes on the Champs-Élysées with a bag dangling from the crook of her arm."

"Designing?" I ask. "Like fashion designing? Are we going to make something for the mannequin to wear? Can I do it? Please?"

Anna shakes her head. "Not by yourself. Not yet. But you are ready to assist. We will make something together. Something beautiful. You will see." Anna walks to the rocking chair and sits down. She interlaces her fingers in her lap. Anna doesn't smile much. The only time I've heard her laugh is when she fake-snapped the sewing machine at me. But a bit of something happy spreads across her face.

"Okay," I say. "What should we do first?"

"First, you should close your eyes and imagine your muse."

Wait, what? I'm finally ready to do something other than sew on fabric scraps and the first step is closing my eyes? I don't want to close my eyes. I want to sit down at the sewing machine and make an actual piece of clothing. I stay standing next to the mannequin, but part of me wants to run out the door and never come back. How can I feel so close to what I want, and also so far?

"Cove," says Anna, her rocking chair creaking as it moves. "Eyes. Closed."

I sigh and close my eyes. There is so much energy in my body that my eyelids quiver and flashes of light show through. Anna must not notice because she says quietly: "Now, picture your muse. See the way she moves. Imagine what she is wearing."

In the beginning, nothing comes. Then, slowly, the blackness gets replaced with blocks of gray that turn into tall buildings. A girl my age appears in front of the buildings. Her arms are swinging and her legs are skipping, but not in a babyish way. Her skirt, which falls to her knees, sways as she moves. Her top takes longer to come, but I begin to see that it is simple and fitted, with a high neck and straps that crisscross down the back.

"You see her, yes?" says Anna.

I nod.

"Good. Now open your eyes. Show me what your muse wants to wear."

I sketch my dress on a piece of paper, just like the contestants do on *Create You*. Anna points out all the details I need to consider—zippers, pleats, seam allowances, linings. I redraw the dress five times. Finally, Anna is satisfied.

"Now," says Anna. "A dress, a coat, a shirt, they are all made of pieces. The pieces must fit together perfectly. Then, and only then, will you have something beautiful."

I think about the Ninas that Toby paints. All the pieces of her in different colors that come together to form her face. The practice work I've been doing with

Jonah, puzzling together cut-up old clothes. The *Create You* episodes I've watched, the fabric scraps I've sewn, the sketches I've drawn. I'm so ready to do this.

I reach under Anna's bed where she says there's a roll of muslin fabric. I unroll the fabric onto the floor. It is dull and stiff. Anna can't bend down, so she points with her finger to where I should cut. I try my best to follow, but it's hard to see how a large circle is going to become the pleated flowing skirt, or how the tapered rectangles will be the high-necked top. On *Create You*, the contestants make quick, clean cuts. When they put their fabric pieces to their mannequin, they fit together perfectly. My pieces are nothing like that. Even with Anna showing me where to pin them together, they gather and droop. The mannequin looks like she is wearing a paper dress that got soaked in the rain. I imagine Benjamin Boyd shaking his head from side to side. I can hear him say, "Cove, what were you *thinking?*"

Instead, I have Anna.

She pushes herself up from the rocking chair using both hands. She moves toward the mannequin, slowly walking around it. "Now," she says, "the real work begins."

"But I just did real work," I say. "It stinks."

"Yes. It does stink."

The word *stink* sounds so wrong coming from Anna's mouth that I smile even though I also want to cry. I can barely look at my dress, it's so bad. I am mad at the fabric for wrinkling. At the pins for slipping. At the cuts for being jagged. At the dress for looking horrible.

I'm mad at Alicia, Paris, Mika, and Carver for making their own sewing look so easy.

I'm mad at Jonah for making me believe I could do this.

I'm mad at Anna for letting me continue while I made a disaster.

And then it's like ocean waves coming at me. I can't stop.

I'm mad at the kids at school who wear shirts just to make other people feel bad.

I'm mad at Sophie and Amelia for barking at me like I'm a dog.

I'm mad at everyone for laughing at me in art class.

I'm mad at Jack for not meeting me at the bus.

I'm mad at Mom for never letting me leave this island.

I'm mad at Nina for not writing me back for two weeks.

I'm mad at Nina for leaving me.

I'm really, really mad at Nina for leaving me all alone.

"Are you finished?" asks Anna.

I'm pretty sure all those thoughts were in my head. But Anna looks like she heard each and every one. I nod. "Yes."

"Good," she says. "This is the beginning. Not the end. You can try again."

"I don't know."

"Luckily for you, Cove, I do. Come back tomorrow. Tomorrow you will see."

20

Saturday morning. Mom is teaching an early yoga class. It's cold, and the truck takes a few tries to start. I pull my legs to my chest as Mom jiggles the key in the ignition. "Thatta girl," says Mom when the engine catches.

The island roads are quiet. The stone walls are dull and gray, no sparkling fairy messages shining through the cracks. We pass the turnoff for Caroline's house. She had a sleepover with Sophie, Amelia, and Molly last night. I heard them planning it at school. They're probably sitting in Caroline's kitchen right now, eating her dad's epic chocolate chip pancakes, laughing at some joke. I bet it's so funny that Caroline spits pancakes across the table. Then they'll laugh even harder.

"Did you remember your homework?" asks Mom when we get to the yoga studio.

I nod.

"Cove, sweetie. Smile for me. Please. We can go to Morning Glory when I'm done teaching. We'll get muffins. I bet they'll be fresh out of the oven."

But we won't laugh so hard that we spit them across the table.

I know that for sure.

I sit on a pile of meditation cushions in the lobby while Mom gets ready for class. The yoga studio smells like sweat and tea tree oil. Students arrive, throwing their shoes in a messy pile, leaving outlines of their bare feet on the shiny wood floor. Mom peeks her head out of the yoga room. She looks around the lobby, then frowns. "See you in an hour," she whispers as she closes the door behind her.

I open my math homework. I doodle around the edges of the paper. In pen. Oops. At least it's just my signature flower that I'm drawing and not something embarrassing, like a dress. A dress that I don't stand a chance of actually being able to sew. Maybe I'll never draw another dress for the rest of my life. Or maybe I'm just taking a break for a day. Or maybe it doesn't matter what I draw because I never actually stood a chance of getting on *Create You*. Maybe applying to the show was just a stupid idea of Jonah's that I was stupid enough to believe was possible.

The lobby door opens. I look up from my paper.

"Cove," says Sean. "Crap. I mean, not crap that it's you. Crap that I'm late."

"She started a while ago," I say.

"Crap." Sean hops on one foot as he tries to pull

off his boot. "It's the snooze button. Gets me every time." Sean switches legs, then adds his boots to the pile of shoes. He walks to the closed studio door. He stares at the door with his hands on his hips. "Yes or no. Yes or no. Crap."

"She doesn't like it when people walk in late to yoga," I say.

"So that's a no vote?"

"But I think she was looking for you before class."

"So that's a yes vote?"

"It's an in-between vote."

"Crap," says Sean.

Watching Sean stare down the door, I realize something. It's like when someone trips and you automatically stop walking to make sure you're still steady. Sean's confusion makes me realize that I was just having a similar conversation in my own head—quit or keep trying? Yes or no? Crap. If I don't go back to Anna's, if I give up, then I'm going to be just like Sean, stuck in this yoga studio day after day, staring at a closed door.

"I change my vote," I say. "I think you should go in."

Sean looks at me over his shoulder and smiles. "I was just thinking the exact same thing. Never know unless you try. Wish me luck, Cove. I'm gonna need it."

Sean opens the door. Mom's voice drifts out over soft chanting music. Sean turns and looks back at me with a fake frightened grin. I give him a thumbs-up. He disappears into the yoga room, closing the door behind him.

I dig in my backpack for a fresh piece of paper. I leave Mom a note. Then I open a different door and walk through.

I've never been to visit Anna in the morning. There's a different smell in the air, a combination of soap and coffee. Walt is in the lobby drinking from a mug. He waves me over. "Well, hello there, Cove," says Walt. "You here for our Anna?"

I nod.

"Didn't see her at breakfast," he says. "She might still be sleeping."

"Should I come back later?"

Walt shakes his head. "A visit is a visit. And Anna loves your visits. Go and check on her. And if she's still sleeping, come on back and visit with me."

Anna is not sleeping. Her bedroom door is open, the light spreading out to the hallway. I hear the steady thud of the sewing machine needle moving up and down. I peek in. Anna is hunched over the sewing machine. Black fabric moves under her hands. Like Alicia on *Create You*, Anna hums as she sews.

I stand still, watching her work. I remember the time Mom dropped me off at Nina's house while Toby was in the middle of painting a Nina. I opened the creaky wooden door to Toby's studio and called Nina's name, but she shook her head with her lips pressed closed. "Sometimes you can't talk when Papa's painting," she explained later. "You'll break the spell and then we won't get strawberry ice cream for dessert."

I don't want to break Anna's spell. I wait until she lifts the presser foot of the sewing machine. She pulls the material free and lays it on the desk. It's only then that I knock on the open door.

"Hi," I say.

"Ah, Cove," says Anna. "Come in." She lifts the black fabric and folds it over one arm. She uses her other arm to push herself to standing. I notice pleats in the black fabric. And crisscrossing straps.

"Is that my design?" I ask.

"Indeed."

Anna hands me the dress. It weighs almost nothing in my hands. At first I'm disappointed that Anna sewed the dress without me. But as I hold up the dress, I'm relieved. The dress is silky and slippery, so different from my muslin mess. The pleats on the skirt are even and the crisscross straps lay flat. It would take me forever to make a dress like this. But Anna did it in just one night. I walk toward the mannequin. Maybe we can go through it piece by piece. Anna can explain all the different steps to me. Except Anna shakes her head. "Not for her," she says. "For you. A gift."

"For me? But it's not supposed to be for me. It's so fancy. And delicate."

"Yes. It is. Try it on. The bathroom is that way."

I go into the bathroom and close the door. I take off my long-sleeved shirt and jeans. I see my reflection in the mirror over the sink. My messy hair. My thick eyebrows. The place where my breasts should be, even though they're not. I am relieved to slip the fabric over my eyes. It blocks my view.

Anna doesn't say anything when I step out. But she does smile. It's not a smile like the girls at school who smile when they're about to do something mean, like bark. It's a smile that comes from behind her wrinkly eyes and spreads across her cheeks. Anna pulls gently on the skirt. She smooths the waist. Then she points to the full-length mirror in the corner of her room and I walk toward it. Anna stands behind me and adjusts the straps on my shoulders.

"Look at you," she says, both our reflections visible in the mirror.

"What?" I whisper.

"So grown-up. So beautiful. It has power, this dress. It's one of them."

"One of what?"

"One of the special ones. Like in the windows of the shops in Paris."

When she puts it on, she becomes someone else. That's what Anna said about the imaginary woman who tries on the beautiful gown. That certain dresses can change people. Maybe that's the way it used to work, or the way it works for others. Like on *Create You* where Mika actually wears caftans and Paris actually wears spikes on her sleeves. But I can't picture it working that way for me. Maybe one day. But not now.

Besides, this dress was meant for my muse, the New York City girl, not me. This dress that feels like swimming underwater at Eel Pond, the way the silk cools my body and the skirt swishes around my legs. I twist a little, feeling the fabric move, seeing myself from a different angle. It makes me jumpy, the way I look in this dress. Because Anna's right, I look different. I feel different. Out of place.

It makes me want to take the dress off. And keep it on.

It makes me want to go back. And race forward.

And somehow, I'm more confused than ever before.

Dear Cove,

I'm sorry I haven't written in a super-long time. I did something really bad. It's almost too bad to write about. But everyone else already knows so I guess you should, too.

Remember how I wrote to you about Minnie's mom's closet and all her fancy clothes? Like those purses with the CC logo? Well, Minnie's mom bought Minnie one of those purses. Minnie started wearing it to school and then all these other girls at school copied her and got the same purse. The purses are super soft and cute and hang on these gold chains that you can wear over your shoulder or across your body. Plus they're the perfect size for cell phones and lip gloss and stuff.

I wanted one of those purses so badly, but my dads said no way. It turns out they are from Chanel. Coco Chanel. The famous fashion designer you were asking about. Dad said bags from Chanel are way way way way too expensive for someone my age. And Papa agreed. But that's not true because all these girls at school have them. It's so unfair.

So one day after school I went down to Papa's studio when he wasn't there. I saw all these paintings of me. Painting after painting of my face and body cut up into tiny shapes like he always does. There was a palette with a huge blob of black paint. Right next to it was a clean brush. I grabbed the brush and painted two Cs over one of his really big paintings. And then I did it to the next one. And the one after that. I don't know what I was thinking. I was just super mad.

Papa was even madder. Madder than he's ever been in his life. But then his stupid agent walked in and said the paintings were brilliant. He said they were symbolic of our generation's obsessions with brands and image and whatever. So they went into his show. They're on the walls of the gallery.

I know that sounds good, but it's not good at all. The gallery printed the story of what happened on the wall right next to where all the paintings hang. Minnie's mom came to the show and took pictures with her phone. Then Minnie texted the pictures to all her friends with a laughing emoji face and now they think I'm a pathetic loser wannabe. Sometimes they make the shape of two Cs with their hands when I walk past.

I had no idea how bad it felt when Sophie and Amelia barked at you. But now I do. Remember that pool in the basement that I told you about? That's where I hang out between classes. All by myself where I don't have to see anyone.

I miss home. I miss the island. I miss you. I hate this stupid city and all these stupid people at school. I wish we'd never moved here. I feel so all alone. Nothing makes sense anymore.

I'm sorry I haven't been writing that much. Just add it to the list of all the bad things I've done since we moved here.

Love,
Nina

Dear Nina,

I just got your letter. Don't worry. I have a plan. I'm going to get on Create You. I'll explain everything later. There's something important I have to do.

Love,
Cove

21

"Is everything okay?" asks Mom. She's rinsing large leaves of kale in the sink.

I shake my head. I'm holding the letters in my hand.

"What happened? Is it Clark? Toby?"

"It's not them. It's Nina. She hates her new school. The kids there are being super mean. I need to send her a letter back. Right now. Can we go to the post office?"

Mom checks her watch. Frowns. But then she says, "Okay, Cove. If it means that much to you, we can make a quick run before dinner. But we have to leave right now."

I run into my room. I fold the letter I just wrote to Nina and slide it into an envelope, sealing it shut. Then I open my desk drawer. The desk is old, the drawer deep and wide. My fingers push past my collection of shaped erasers, my old doodles, and the Popsicle-stick people that Nina and I used to make with Toby. I feel a stack of paper at the back, but I'm searching for something specific: the Create You application that Jonah printed out for me weeks ago. I shoved it in the back of my desk drawer where Mom wouldn't find it. Just like I hung Anna's black dress, the one she made for me, in the way back of my closet.

I filled out the basics of the Create You application as soon as I got it—name, age, address. But the rest is still blank. Now, with my sealed letter to Nina in front of me and the application in my hand, I know what I *should* do. I should change my mind. Tear the letter in two, crumple the application into a paper ball, and throw them both away. I picture the letter and the application floating into my trash can, where they would land with hardly a sound.

But I'm tired of not making a sound. I'm tired of ignoring the barking and the shirts. I'm tired of signing petitions because I'm scared not to. I think about Nina's words: *Nothing makes sense anymore*. She's right. Nothing makes sense. No one else is following the rules. Rules like best friends stay together, students listen to teachers, and trying your best is all you can do. Why should I be the only one?

I grab a pen. On the application there are several blank lines underneath the words "Personal Statement." I figure a personal statement is like the personal narrative assignment we did in school last year. A paragraph about who you are. Before I can worry about what I want to write or what I should write, I begin.

My name is Cove Bernstein and I live on Martha's Vineyard. I've lived here my entire life and I've never left. Not even once. A few months ago my best friend moved to New York City. I started watching Create You because it made me feel closer to her. But then I started to love the show. I love how the contestants are all so different. I love how they imagine something and bring it to life. Where I live, you can only be one kind of person. And you don't even get to decide for yourself who that person is. It feels like other people decide for you. I don't know if that makes sense. I guess nothing makes sense anymore. I just really need to get on Create You. I'll try my best to be a really good contestant.

"Cove," calls Mom. "We've gotta go if you want to get to the post office before it closes."

"Coming!" I call back.

I put down my pen. Below the blank lines for the personal statement is a reminder to include an original sewing sample with the application. I don't have time to check over my personal statement. And I don't have time to think through what I do next.

I just do it.

With shaky hands, I reach into the back of my closet.

I slide the black dress off its hanger.

And I hope that Anna will understand why.

22

"**H**ey," I say to Jack on Tuesday. We're back in art class drawing ideas for our scarecrows. I haven't seen Jack since art class last week, so I'm surprised when he chooses the spot next to me on the floor. He lays on his side so the chains from his pocket are touching the ground. There are no new blue tabs.

"*Libre, libre,*" says Ms. Ratowski as she walks around the room in her black clogs. "That's Spanish for 'free.' Free those ideas and let them flow."

"Good luck with that," whispers Jack. "This place

is where ideas go to die. Unless you can buy them off Amazon with your parents' credit card."

I know he's talking about the STAY AWAY FROM US shirts because he nods at Sophie and Amelia, who are sitting on the floor in the opposite corner of the art room. They're wearing the shirts. They don't wear them every day anymore, more like twice a week. But they must plan in advance because they always wear them on the same days. Molly's sitting with them, but she's not wearing her shirt today.

"Sorry I've been MIA," says Jack.

"It's okay," I say.

"It's not you. I've just been busy."

I think Jack's trying to start a conversation with me because he looks like he's about to say more. Even though a few days ago I would have been relieved that things were back to normal, today I'm having trouble concentrating. I've never done anything like what I did yesterday, and it's all I can think about.

The padded envelope with Anna's black dress inside.

The separate letter to Nina beside it.

The postman smiling as he stamped both envelopes and dropped them in a giant mail crate behind the counter.

At night I couldn't fall asleep. I couldn't get these images out of my brain. I stayed up late enough to hear Sean come over to our house. I heard him and Mom fighting. Not about Sean being late to yoga, but about how Sean wants Mom to travel with him off island. "Anywhere," he said. "We could go anywhere. Cove, too. You can't spend the rest of your life hiding away here trying to protect her from some imaginary trauma. It's no way to live."

"You're so naive," Mom said back. "And stupid. And irresponsible."

Lying in bed, Mom's angry words made me feel better. I could pretend that they were meant for me.

That Mom knew what I'd done and would help me fix it once she calmed down.

But now, in daylight, I realize that I'm in this all alone.

"Whatcha got there, Cove?" asks Ms. Ratowski. She crouches down to get a closer look at my paper. "Hmm. We've seen witches before. You're such a talented artist. You've got more to give than that. I know you do. Draw deep."

I look down at my paper and realize that I've been drawing a black dress. It's the same shape as Anna's dress, but in chunky marker it does look witchy. The pleats make the skirt look tattered.

"It's not that bad," says Jack.

"Thanks," I say. "But it's pretty bad."

"You know, you can totally win this scarecrow designing contest if you want to," says Jack.

"No, I can't."

"Why not? You're still sewing with Anna, right?

And watching *Create You?* You probably know more about fashion design than anyone in this school."

"This isn't *fashion* design," I say. "It's a stuffed scarecrow contest. And I don't even have a good idea." I put my black marker down and it rolls across the room. I don't try to go after it.

Then something pops into my head. A scene from a *Create You* episode where the contestants had to pick the fairy tale princess they most admire and create a gown for her to wear. There was this one scene of Mika in the aisle of a fabric store. She was walking down a row of silks, running her finger across the bolts of fabric when she started to cry. Martina Velez came up to her. "What's wrong?" she asked. "This isn't me," said Mika. "I'm a beach girl; I don't even like princesses. I don't have any ideas." Martina Velez put her hands on Mika's shoulders and said, "Mika, just be yourself, believe in yourself, and the ideas will come."

I could tell that Mika didn't really believe her, but

Martina Velez is so kind that Mika nodded anyway. Then the camera shifted to Carver, who was happily walking down the aisles, tossing supplies like beads and feathers and ribbon into his basket. For just one second, in the corner of the screen, Mika turned on her heels and walked away from the fancy silks toward the aisle that had funky print fabrics. It took a long time before the camera showed her again. This time, she was back in the sewing room draping a combination of fabrics across her mannequin. There were all kinds of colors, from neon green to fuchsia to tangerine to electric pink. When Martina Velez and Benjamin Boyd got to Mika's work area, Martina Velez smiled. She examined Mika's mannequin. Then she said in her happy Martina Velez way, "See, Mika, you just had to believe in you."

"Hey, Cove," says a voice above me. It's Molly. She's holding the black marker. I have no idea how long she's been standing there. "I think this is yours," says Molly as she hands me the marker. "It rolled across the room."

"Thanks," I say.

Molly pauses. She looks like she's at a busy street, unsure of when the traffic will stop to let her cross.

"Do you guys mind if I sit here for a sec?" she says. "I just need a change."

Jack looks at me with a raised eyebrow. He's about to shake his head when I say, "Sure, join us."

Ms. Ratowski is not Martina Velez or Benjamin Boyd.

The art room at Martha's Vineyard Middle School is not a sewing room in New York City.

I am not Mika.

But an idea comes.

And I know exactly what to do.

Dear Cove Bernstein,

Congratulations! You have been selected to proceed to the second phase of the *Create You* application process. Every season we get hundreds of applications from talented young designers, but only the top thirty are chosen to advance to this exciting next step. For the second phase of the application, we will be sending a local camera crew to your home to conduct an on-screen interview. Details on dates and scheduling will be determined in the following weeks.

Sincerely,

The *Create You* Team

Cove—Martina and I personally review all the applications and the quality of your dress blew both of us away. It's rare to see so much craftsmanship and attention to detail in a young sewer. I also read your personal statement, and it brought back memories of how I felt growing up. From one artist to another, please don't let anyone tell you who you are. Only you get to decide that. Best wishes for your on-camera interview. Martina and I are rooting for you!

—Benjamin Boyd

23

The letter from *Create You* weighs a ton. It is everything I've done wrong and everything I wanted to do right. Benjamin Boyd's note makes me feel worse, not better. His words are so nice. I just wish that I had actually earned them.

I don't tell anyone about the letter. One good thing about your best friend moving away and the one new friend you've made acting distant is there's no one to notice that you're not talking. That the teacher asks you to stay after class because you haven't turned in your homework. That your eyes are red from lying awake at night and swollen from crying. That when someone barks at you in the hallway, you don't flinch because you barely hear the sound.

But after a few days, I can't take it anymore. I need someone to know what I've done.

I think about telling Mom. But I don't want to hear about the divine wisdom of the universe and how everything happens for a reason. I don't want to hear the story of my name, the little girl on the safe ocean cove. Because that girl is gone. Long gone.

I think about telling Jack. But I don't want anyone at school to know. He's too close.

I think about telling Nina. She's too far away.

I think about telling Anna. But I'm worried she'll be mad. Furious.

But there is someone who will understand: Jonah.

I take the bus to Sal's.

There's the same tinkling bell over the front door. The same dust motes in the air. The same smell of old clothes and older carpet. But instead of Jonah, Sal is standing behind the front desk.

"Cove Bear!" he calls, taking off his glasses. "I've missed you! Look how you've grown in just a few weeks!"

He opens his thick arms to give me a hug. I know exactly how his arms will feel and I want to rush into them. I want to be the little girl who falls madly in love with a Care Bear shirt. The one who feels special simply because Sal saved her a brown paper bag full of clothes that someone else no longer wanted.

Instead, tears fill my eyes.

"Cove Bear, what's wrong? You miss me that much?"

I wipe my eyes. "Where's Jonah?"

Sal raises his arms and shrugs his shoulders. "I called a few days ago to let him know that I was coming back. Then I got a message yesterday that he had left the island on the last ferry. He said something about forwarding his last paycheck. At least, that's what I thought he said. He talks so fast, that Jonah. I have trouble understanding everything he's saying. But I did find this note on the counter. Addressed to you."

"Me?"

"Do you know any other Cove on this island?"

I shake my head and Sal hands me a folded note with my name on it. It's written on a strip of paper from the cash register, long and narrow.

Cove—I GOT THE E-MAIL! I'm off the wait list and ready to unleash my pen on the world! Take cover, everyone! I wish I could say good-bye in person, but I gotta fly. At the risk of getting all guru on you, always remember how much you rock. School can be bananas, and I know it doesn't always feel like it, but you're going to make it through. There's light at the end of the tunnel, Covinator. Take it from someone who's made it to the other side.

Keep drawing. Keep creating. Keep being you.

Peace out.

Jonah

"Everything okay?" asks Sal.

"Yeah," I say, even though it's not. The store feels too quiet without Jonah. And when I step outside, the whole island will feel too quiet. The feeling will be in the air, on the sandy beaches, covering my skin. One more person gone.

I put Jonah's note in my back pocket.

Right next to the letter from *Create You.*

24

The next morning crushed wet leaves from the soles of everyone's shoes stick to the school hallways. It's raining, and the entire island feels soggy. The bottom of my jeans are still wet as I find a seat toward the back of the auditorium. We don't normally have morning assembly on Thursday, but today there was a large sign in the front hall instructing everyone to go straight to the auditorium instead of homeroom.

"Psst," says a voice behind me.

I turn. It's Jack.

"Feels like the good old days," he says.

We are sitting in the same seats as the first time we spoke. He's even sitting in the exact same way, with his arms across the backs of the chairs on either side of him. It feels like more than just a few weeks have passed. Back then, I thought the worst had already happened. Nina had moved away. I had no idea how much trickier it was going to get.

I get out of my seat and move to Jack's row. "Where have you been?" I ask.

"Me? Nowhere." He shakes his head back and forth, but I feel like he's hiding something.

"Then why haven't I seen you at school in days?"

"I've been busy."

"Busy doing what, dumpster diving? Every single day? Then why don't you have anything new?" I nod toward the chains on his jeans. There's still only one blue tab.

Jack turns to face me and his chains clink against the metal side of the seat. His downcast eyes tell me the most important thing—he doesn't want to hurt my feelings.

"Just tell me the truth, Jack. Please."

"Fine," says Jack. "I've been off island meeting with this private school advisor in Boston. My mom's project here is only a year, and then we're going to be moving. Again. I have to take this test to apply to schools for next year, and my mom's freaking out because my scores stink. She doesn't know where we're going next, but she says no matter what, I need to have options." Jack talks fast, like the words are dominos falling onto each other. Words that I can almost feel hit me.

"Why didn't you tell me?"

"I was going to. That day at Sal's. But then that dude Jonah pulled me aside when you were in the bathroom and said how psyched he was that I had come to hang out. He seemed like he was worried about you or something. And I don't know. I just didn't get around to saying anything."

"Because you felt sorry for me? Is that what you mean?"

"No, that's not why. I swear."

"Then why? It doesn't make any sense."

"Maybe it's not all about you, Cove. Maybe *I* didn't feel like talking about it. I've learned some things, you know. Like it doesn't do any good to tell people you're leaving when it feels like you only just got someplace and you don't even know where you're going next. Maybe my mom is cool with spending her life going to good-bye parties where people give you hugs and promise to keep in touch even though they know, and you know, that it's all a lie. But not me. Why does everyone need to make such a big deal about everything? You were happy and Jonah was happy, and what? I'm just going to crash the party and be like, check ya later, everyone? I'm leaving again and I need you all to know?"

Principal Finnery walks onstage before I can answer. She does the bunny ears thing, and everyone begins to quiet down. But I don't hear what Principal Finnery is saying. All I can think about is Jack. I never thought of Jack as caring about what other people think. But now I start to wonder, maybe he didn't want to be the guy standing far away from the four-square court. Or the one sitting with an empty seat on either side of him. The one moving from place to place all the time, never knowing where he's going next.

But no matter how I look at it, one thing is clear: Everyone leaves.

Nina left because she had to.

Jonah left because he wanted to.

And Jack's going to leave, too. It's only a matter of time.

I notice people turning their heads. They are shifting in their seats. Ms. Ratowski is up on stage in her clogs and paint-stained jeans. She is squinting as she looks out at the rows of seats. For some reason, everyone is clapping. Some kids even start to pump their arms and howl like wolves.

Jack leans over and taps me on the shoulder. "Earth to Cove," he says. "They're calling your name."

25

The lights onstage are bright. They make me squint, just like Ms. Ratowski. So I look down at the wood planks of the stage instead of out at the seats. Also, my whole body is shaking, and looking down makes it easier to pretend that I'm not standing in front of the entire school. That there aren't hundreds of voices chanting my name. *Cove! Cove! Cove!* Principal Finnery smiles as she clicks a remote in her hand. A picture of my scarecrow design glows on the screen behind us. Up close, this large, the design looks nothing like the smooth and flowing fashion sketches on *Create You.*

It's a simple outline in black marker of a white T-shirt, the kind a little kid would draw on her first attempt at a self-portrait. Square sleeves, straight bottom, curved neckline.

But it's not the shirt that's making people cheer. It's the two words written on it: JOIN US. I drew the letters in all caps, large and thick, so they really pop against the white. They're impossible to ignore.

"This," says Principal Finnery, "is the design that will be representing our school at the Scarecrow Stroll. Congratulations, Cove. Your submission was unanimously chosen by the entire staff. Well done."

More cheers. More chanting. It's hard to know what to do with my body, with my face. I'm relieved to feel Ms. Ratowski's hand on my back directing me off the side of the stage. It's only once we get past the thick curtains blocking the audience's view that I breathe.

"I'm so proud of you, Cove," says Ms. Ratowski. "Moments like this are why art exists. They inspire people to examine themselves and the world they live in. You made that happen, all by yourself. Well done. *Complimenti!*"

"Thanks," I say.

"And now you get to do the most fun part—create! Are you free after school today?"

I nod. I was planning to go to Anna's this afternoon. To confess what I'd done. But I'm so shocked by what just happened that I don't think fast enough to explain that to Ms. Ratowski.

"Great," says Ms. Ratowski. "We just found out that the Scarecrow Stroll was pushed up to this Saturday because after that it's supposed to rain for the rest of the week. Some late-season hurricane. *¡Dios mío!* What do people think, that these scarecrows create themselves? How about you gather some friends and meet me in the art room after dismissal. I already have all the supplies. I just need some nimble art-loving fingers."

🌱 🌱 🌱

"Man, this hay is sharp," I hear Jack say. He and Charlotte M. are in the hallway stuffing straw into the scarecrow body. Molly and I are inside the art room cutting out letters. Ms. Ratowski is in the parking lot folding down the seats of her minivan so we can transport the scarecrow without smushing it.

"It's just hay," says Charlotte. "Horses eat it all day long."

"Yeah, well, horses must be pretty freaking tough," says Jack.

"Tougher than you," says Charlotte.

Molly and I laugh.

"Anna's going to be so proud of you," says Molly as she carefully cuts an S out of fabric. "Maybe one of our moms can give her a ride to the Scarecrow Stroll."

"Maybe," I say.

"Do you think Anna needs a wheelchair? I've always wanted to push one. I can't tell if they're heavy like a wheelbarrow or light like a stroller. Do you think that's a weird thing to think about?"

I don't answer. I'm too busy thinking that pride is the last thing Anna will feel once she finds out what I did with the black dress.

Molly looks up from her cutting. "What's wrong, Cove? Is it me? Did Ms. Ratowski force you to include me today?"

"What? No."

"I'm so sorry, Cove. I never should have worn one of the shirts. Sophie and Amelia grabbed me as I was walking into the back-to-school picnic. They had an extra shirt and told me to put it on. They said if I wore the shirt, they would invite me to all their sleepovers and make it the best year ever. I saw what the shirt said, but I didn't really think about it until it was too late. I just wanted . . . I wanted the year to be good, you know? That's all I was thinking about. Or not even good, more like not awful. Does that make sense?"

"Yeah," I say. "It does." But there's something I

need to know. "Why did you keep wearing the shirt? After the picnic was over?"

"Because it worked," says Molly. "They did invite me to sleepovers and movies and all that stuff."

"I heard about the sleepover at Caroline's house. With her dad's epic chocolate chip pancakes."

"I didn't go. No epic pancakes for me."

"Why not?"

Molly shrugs. "I didn't feel like it. Everything is always such a big deal with them. Like Sophie wouldn't let us tuck in the shirts because that wrinkled the letters and made the words hard to read. And then once other people started wearing the shirts, Amelia decided that we should all wear matching red nail polish so that everyone would know we went together as a group. I hate nail polish. It chips and then it makes me want to scratch my fingernails off. I guess I just got tired of not having fun. This," she motions to the messy art room, "is way more fun."

I look at the floor. It's a mess. A mess of fabric scraps and thread and random bits of straw. I picture Martina Velez's hot pink high heels stomping across it. I picture Benjamin Boyd throwing his leather jacket over a paint-splattered stool. In some strange way, what I'm doing right now is pretty close to *Create You*.

Jack bursts into the art room, dragging the naked scarecrow behind him. "I am done with straw!" he says. "This guy is as stuffed as he's going to get. Give me something else to do. Anything else."

Maybe it's the ghosts of Martina Velez and Benjamin Boyd floating in the air, but I know just what the scarecrow needs to look its best. "Jack," I say. "Quick. Before they empty all the trash cans. He needs a chain. Or maybe two."

Jack nods. "On it. Come on, Charlotte. I'll show you just how tough I really am. You ever gone dumpster diving before?"

26

My scarecrow is placed on Dock Street in Edgartown, across the street from Candies from Heaven, where Nina and I used to spend our money on Pop Rocks and gummy worms. Jack, Molly, Charlotte M., and I style the scarecrow perfectly. We place him on a bench, so his arms are open and hanging on either side of the backrest, just like Jack on the first day I met him. Ms. Ratowski stopped by Sal's and picked up an old pair of jeans that we slid over the scarecrow's legs. Jack and Charlotte M.'s two chains run from the scarecrow's belt loop to his pocket.

And the shirt. The JOIN US shirt is perfect. The letters are wobbly and Anna would never approve of the stitches—they're way too uneven—but the message is clear.

Anyone who wants to sit next to our scarecrow is more than welcome.

"Cove, I'm just so proud of you," says Mom. "I remember when you were that little spirit kicking around inside my belly and it feels like all my hopes for you have come true. You're a gorgeous being, Cove. A blessing."

Mom pulls me into her arms and that's when I lose it. I almost lost it two nights ago, when I got home from school after making my scarecrow and my fingers were stinging with needle pricks. I almost lost it this morning when I saw a new letter from *Create You* in a stack of unread mail on the kitchen table. I almost lost it an hour ago when a photographer from *The Vineyard Gazette* took a picture of me with my scarecrow that

Molly and Jack photobombed. The photographer said it was the best picture he's taken all year and that it's definitely going to run on the front page.

All those almosts pile up inside me until there's no more space. "Mom," I say into her chest because I don't have the courage to say it to her face. "I did something really, really bad and I need to fix it."

Anna isn't in the lobby when I get there. I look in the common room with its plaid sofas and the dining room where circular tables are set with silverware and folded napkins. I see Walt shuffling down a hallway using his walker.

"Walt," I yell, running toward him.

"Hey there, child," he says. "You scared me. Not much running happens 'round these parts."

"Sorry," I say. "It's just, I'm looking for Anna. Have you seen her?"

"Anna?" Walt leans on his walker and lifts one

hand as if he wants to reach out and touch me. But his hand trembles and he puts it back down. "Oh, child, she moved on, our Anna. Just one night ago. It was her time."

"Moved on? Where? Where did she move to?" Even as I wait for Walt to say another room, or another floor, I know what he means. It's in the way his entire body sags. Anna's moved on to a place that she can't come back from.

"Come," says Walt.

I follow him to Anna's room. There are cardboard boxes on the bed and the closet door is wide open. A woman wearing a navy-blue sweater peeks out of the closet and smiles. She stands up straight, like a teacher in front of a class. "Let me guess," she says. "You must be Cove."

"How do you know my name?"

"Anna talked about you all the time. In fact, the last time we spoke, Anna mentioned staying up all night to finish sewing a dress for you. When I told her not to forget about her beauty sleep, she shushed me right up. Said nothing mattered except making you the perfect dress, so that you'd always have something to remember her by."

"Anna said that?"

The woman nods. "And that she hoped she had sewn enough love into the seams to last you the rest of your life. I hear a lot of things in my line of work, but that one hit me right here." She puts her hand over her heart.

It hits me, too. "Who are you?" I ask.

"I'm Andrea, her social worker."

"Social worker?"

Andrea nods. "We check on folks who need to be checked on. Make sure they're getting the help they need."

Maybe I've got it all wrong. Maybe Anna did just move to another floor. Like in a wheelchair or something.

"So where is she?" I ask.

Andrea reaches out and puts her hand on my shoulder. Her fingers feel like octopus tentacles latching onto me and I want to peel them off, one by one. "Oh, sweetie, I'm sorry. I didn't mean to imply . . . Anna's dead. She died peacefully in her sleep. But she left you something." Andrea walks over to Anna's desk and nods to the sewing machine. "She wanted you to have this."

The sewing machine looks lonely. And sad. Like something that's lost.

It looks how I feel.

Dear Benjamin Boyd and Martina Velez,

I am writing because I have a confession about the black dress that you liked so much. I didn't sew it. Someone else did. Her name was Anna and she was an amazing seamstress. You would have loved her (only she was WAY too old to be on Create You). Anna was teaching me to sew, but no matter how hard I tried, I couldn't sew like she did. So I made a big mistake and I sent the dress that Anna sewed as part of my application.

Anna died a few days ago, before I got up the courage to tell her what I did. Now I can't tell her I'm sorry for pretending that I sewed her dress. It's too late. So I'm telling you instead. I got your letter, and you don't need to send a camera crew to interview me because I don't deserve to be on Create You. But I have one big favor to ask. Would you mind mailing the black dress back to me? I'd really like to see it again.

I also wanted to send you something that I did sew

all by myself. I promise. It's just letters on a shirt and not good enough to get me on *Create You*, but I hope you like it. I think Anna would be proud of it even if some of the stitches are crooked. She really hated crooked stitches.

Sincerely,

Cove Bernstein

P.S. Sorry if the shirt smells like straw. I didn't have time to wash it. Long story.

Six Months Later

April

The lights on the television set are super bright, but I've gotten used to bright lights. On Martha's Vineyard, night means darkness sliced with slivers of clear moons and twinkles of bright stars. Here in New York City, there are tons of lights all the time. They glow in all different colors, sizes, and shapes. There are headlights from cars, billboards flashing ads in neon, and tall buildings lit up from within. When I first got here, I felt like I had to squint. Just like when I stood onstage at school. But then I got used to the lights.

Nina squeezes my hand as we stand, waiting. "This is so exciting!" she says. "I've never been on the set of a real TV show!" Her hand in my hand swings back and forth. Back and forth. I'm too nervous to speak. Or smile. In just a few minutes, a producer wearing a gray sweatshirt and headset is going to give me a hand signal. I'm going to walk down a narrow hallway to stand next to Benjamin Boyd and Martina Velez and announce the next *Create You* challenge—to design a shirt that sparks kindness. I'm supposed to tell the contestants the story of my scarecrow.

I'm supposed to tell everyone.

I've never been this nervous in my entire life. There are people and cameras everywhere, all waiting to start recording. In a few weeks the show is going to play on a big screen in the school auditorium. Principal Finnery invited all the residents of the Vineyard Senior Center to come. We got to spend an entire art class with Ms. Ratowski handwriting invitations. Sophie and Amelia wrote a petition to protest old people taking up the front row seats and crowding the hallways with their wheelchairs and walkers, but no one signed. Not one single person. When Principal Finnery heard about the petition, she gave Sophie and Amelia five afternoons of trash pick-up duty for violating the updated student code of conduct. Trash pick-up duty is a new job. For some reason students have started digging around in trash cans and dumpsters. The teachers can't figure out what to do about it.

I hope Jack will still be at school when the show plays. I picture him sitting with his arms spread wide. Maybe Molly and I will sit next to him. Or Charlotte M. Or Walt.

I peek around the corner to check on Mom. She's sitting with Sean, Toby, and Clark in a small room with television screens on the walls. The screens show different angles of the *Create You* stage where Martina Velez is stretching her neck and Benjamin Boyd is smoothing the sleeves of his leather jacket. Mom didn't want me to go to New York City, but when I got the invitation, all expenses paid, I told her I was going with or without her.

"But it would be much better if you came with me," I said.

"I don't know, Cove," said Mom. "It's a lot. It's more than you could ever imagine."

"Remember what you always say about the traffic, or the rain, or anything bad?" I said. "That it'll pass? How about we stop waiting for everything to pass. How about we open an umbrella and walk in it?"

Sean clapped when I said that. "I've been trying to tell your mom that exact same thing for weeks, Cove. Only, kudos, kid, you said it way better."

"Please, Mom," I said. "We'll still be us. We'll just be us in New York City."

Mom looked at me, laughing and crying at the same time, the beaded bracelets on her wrist clanking as she raised her hand to wipe her eyes. She pulled me onto her lap, where I don't fit anymore. She buried her nose in my hair. "Okay, Cove," she whispered. "I'll go. We'll go together."

In the room with all the television screens, Sean puts his arm across Mom's shoulders. His arm with all the numbers representing the places he's been.

40.759011, -73.984472. That's the number for New York City. Nina looked it up on her phone last night when I told her about Sean and his tattoos.

Nina smiles at me. I think about the spinning wheel at the playground next to the Artists Market. How Nina and I would lay back and look up at the clouds. How we would spin into the same person, our bodies and thoughts whirling together so that we could read each other's minds.

Now we are still.

There is no bright blue sky above us, no dirt below us.

But we are friends. Always and forever. She can read my thoughts.

I'm scared.

I know you are. But you're also brave. You can do this. I'll be right here when you're done.

The producer wearing the gray sweatshirt and headset walks toward us.

I take a deep breath. Anna's black dress brushes against my legs.

The producer counts down with his fingers. Five. Four. Three. Two. One. He points to me and I let go of Nina's hand.

I take one step. Then two. Then three.

I walk toward the bright lights.

I tell my story.

Acknowledgments

Thank you to my agent, Alexander Slater. Your belief in this story and my voice changed everything. I am so grateful for your endless support.

Thank you to my editor, Martha Mihalick, for loving Cove and guiding her story with enormous skill and care. It is an honor and privilege to work with you.

And to everyone at Greenwillow Books—Virginia Duncan, Katherine Heit, Tim Smith, Sylvie Le Floc'h, Vaishali Nayak, Kadeen Griffiths, and Kristopher Kam. Thank you for adding this novel to your incredible collection of children's literature. And to Merillee Liddiard, for the beautiful art.

Thank you to Dani Shapiro for your kindness and encouragement when I was full of doubt. To Steve and Amy Blecher for years of love, and to Jack and Pamela Ende for a lifetime of love.

To my daughters: Ella, Liv, and Aven. Thank you for cheering me on all these years, for reading all my stories, and for inspiring me with your joy. I write with you three girls in my head and in my heart.

Most of all, thank you to my husband, Jeff. For absolutely everything. None of this would be possible without you.

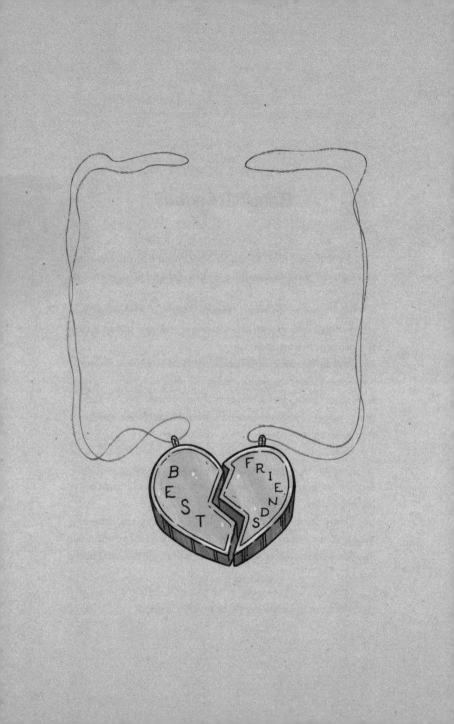

WHEN LIFE GETS COMPLICATED,
CAN TWO UNLIKELY FRIENDS HELP
EACH OTHER THROUGH IT?
READ ON FOR AN EXCERPT OF
STICK WITH ME, BY JENNIFER BLECHER

Stick
with
Me

Friends forever?
Or for never?

JENNIFER BLECHER

WHEN LIFE GETS COMPLICATED,
CAN TWO UNLIKELY FRIENDS HELP
EACH OTHER THROUGH IT?
READ ON FOR AN EXCERPT OF
STICK WITH ME, BY JENNIFER BLECHER

Stick

with

Me

Friends forever?
Or for never?

JENNIFER BLECHER

THE OPPOSITE OF IZZY

When Izzy was little, she was obsessed with opposites. Not regular opposites, like left and right. Happy and sad. Good and bad. She wasn't the kind of kid who occasionally walked down the sidewalk backward. Instead, Izzy blew milk out of a straw. She ate cereal with a fork. She wore her backpack on her stomach every single day of preschool.

It didn't make any sense.

But back then, making sense didn't matter. Izzy could color only the background of a coloring page, and her teacher would smile and say, "What a unique way to look at that picture, Izzy. You did such a nice job coloring *outside* the lines."

And it wasn't just teachers. No one in her family cared about making sense. If Izzy danced around the kitchen with underwear on her head, there was an excellent chance that her parents would laugh. Or that her older brother Nate would twirl her down the hallway.

But now Izzy was twelve. And that kind of stuff wasn't funny anymore; it was embarrassing. Izzy no longer wanted to be different from everyone else.

She wanted the opposite.

As Izzy sat at her desk watching her friend Phoebe, she got a familiar feeling, like things were the opposite of how they were supposed to be. Only the feeling didn't make Izzy smile or laugh. It made her worry about what was going to happen next.

"I'm not sure I get it," said Phoebe. Phoebe was laying on Izzy's bed. Her feet swayed in the air and her head rested in her palms. Four beaded bracelets slid halfway down Phoebe's arm. They were the same bracelets that Daphne Toll, the most popular girl in class, had started wearing a few months ago.

There were real bracelets and there were fake bracelets. The real bracelets were made of colored stones threaded on a thick elastic band. The fake bracelets looked exactly the same, but instead of stones, they were made with heavy plastic beads. The only way to tell which bracelets were real and which were fake was to listen to the sound the bracelets made when they hit one another or a hard surface.

Daphne's bracelets were real. Izzy sat next to Daphne in English and had to listen as Daphne clacked her bracelets together during silent reading time. Phoebe's bracelets were fake. Phoebe's mom had bought them in the "buy three, get one free" section at Glitz.

But Izzy had never told anyone that. And neither had Phoebe.

Real and fake. Opposites.

"Earth to Izzy," said Phoebe. She waved her hand with the bracelets back and forth. "Hel-lo."

"Sorry," said Izzy. "What'd you say?"

"I said, I don't get this sticker door. What's the point? What were we *thinking*?" Phoebe nodded toward the back of Izzy's bedroom door. It was covered with hundreds of stickers. There were heart stickers, puppy stickers, and unicorn stickers. There was a winding path of stars, fuzzy ducks wearing red rain boots, and grinning cows jumping over full moons. Around the doorknob was a swirl of whales, seahorses, and sharks. Toward the top of the door were smiling pieces of sushi, old-fashioned dolls wearing lace bonnets, and neon skulls with empty eye sockets. The bottom of the door was lined with neat rows of emoji stickers.

Izzy and Phoebe used to stare at the masterpiece that they'd created together and imagine stories about the lives of the stickers. *Green neon skull and doll in a lace bonnet had a baby named poop emoji.* That kind of thing.

Izzy shrugged. "We were thinking that it was fun?"

"I guess," said Phoebe. "But I just don't get it anymore. I don't get the point."

"There wasn't a point."

"There has to be a point, Izzy. Otherwise, what's the point?"

This was how Phoebe spoke now that she hung out with Daphne and all her popular friends. Now that she wore a stack of bracelets on her wrist and sat at Daphne's table in the cafeteria, draping her arms and legs over Daphne so that everyone could see how deeply connected they were. Now that she spun her lacrosse stick in her hand as she walked to the playing fields for practice, her ponytail held back with a navy-blue elastic headband just like every other girl on the team.

Everything had to *mean* something. And the most annoying part was, Phoebe never knew what anything meant. She just liked to wonder about it.

Like what did it *mean* that Zach bumped into her when Phoebe was putting away her iPad in science? What did it *mean* that Serena went to Dr. Forte's office on Thursday afternoon? What did it *mean* that Mr. Blair picked Phoebe last to give her presentation in English?

Here's what Izzy wanted to know: What did it *mean*

that Phoebe, who'd had tons of sleepovers in Izzy's bedroom, was looking around the room like she'd never seen it before? What did it *mean* that watching Phoebe pull at the frayed knees of her jeans made Izzy wonder if her splatter-paint leggings were babyish? What did it *mean* that having Phoebe close by made Izzy feel lonelier than actually being alone?

Phoebe sat up on Izzy's bed and crossed her legs. Her bare knee popped through the hole in her jeans. "Should we find our moms?" Phoebe asked. "They're probably done talking by now."

So I can finally go home. Those were the words Phoebe didn't say. Although they both knew that the only reason Phoebe was at Izzy's house was because their moms wanted to catch up over a cup of tea.

Phoebe's mom and Izzy's mom were best friends. Sometimes Izzy imagined their moms like a drawing in a picture book: two smiling girls holding hands against a white background with the words BEST FRIENDS written underneath in thick black text. That's all the page would say, as if having a best friend was the simplest thing in the world. As if everyone had a best friend necklace from Glitz, the kind with two jagged half hearts on separate chains that fit together to make a whole.

When they were little, Phoebe and Izzy had been best friends, too. They had half-heart necklaces. They'd gone to the mall and picked them out before their first day of kindergarten. Their moms took their picture, told them how adorable they were, and bought them strawberry ice cream cones to celebrate. Because that's how things worked back then. Necklaces formed hearts. There weren't real hearts and fake hearts. There were just two halves that fit together to make a whole.

Izzy didn't know exactly when everything changed, or why. But she was certain that two simple words no longer described her and Phoebe. Their friendship wasn't just building fairy houses, or performing dance routines on summer nights while their parents ate dinner in the backyard, or making slime creations speckled with silver glitter. It was birthday parties where Izzy was no longer the one seated right next to Phoebe when Phoebe blew out the candles on her cake, school pickups where Phoebe piled into cars heading to houses that Izzy had never been invited to, and beaded bracelets and lacrosse team headbands that Phoebe wore daily and Izzy did not own.

That this change had happened slowly didn't make it any less confusing. If anything, Izzy wished that there had been something specific, like when they were little and Izzy had stuck a heart sticker on the belly of Phoebe's stuffed bunny named Carrot because she thought it would make Phoebe happy. Phoebe had been the opposite of happy, especially when she ripped the sticker off and discovered that it had left behind a sticky gray goo that matted Carrot's pink fur. As Phoebe sat on the kitchen floor with tears and snot streaming down her face, Izzy and her mom had soaked Carrot in a bucket of warm soapy water until the sticker goo came off. Then Izzy and Phoebe spent the rest of the day playing animal spa, bathing their favorite stuffed animals and laying them in the sun to dry.

By dinnertime, they were begging their moms to let them have a sleepover.

Izzy almost smiled, remembering how they brought their stuffed animals ripe blueberries stacked onto toothpicks and bowed as they presented the delicate treats. But then Izzy realized that she had no idea if Phoebe still slept with Carrot tucked under her arm, if Phoebe still chewed on Carrot's long ears when she was nervous, or threw Carrot against the wall when she was frustrated. How long had it been since Izzy had seen Carrot's large feet and black stitched grin? Months? Maybe even a whole year?

Phoebe rolled off Izzy's bed, examined her nails, and sighed. "Come on," she said. "Let's go."

"One sec," said Izzy. She swiveled her chair so that her back was to Phoebe and glanced at the drawer of her desk. Her half of their jagged heart necklace was inside. But there was something else inside, too. A stack of papers that Izzy didn't want Phoebe, or anyone else, to see.

"Come on, Iz," said Phoebe. "I'm starving."

A piece of striped washi tape was stuck across the panel of the drawer, sealing it shut. The top edge of the tape was beginning to curl away and Izzy was tempted to reach out and fix it. But there was no way to do that without Phoebe noticing. Phoebe would wonder what the tape *meant*.

And even Phoebe was smart enough to know the answer.

Izzy stood up and followed Phoebe out of her bedroom toward the back stairway. As they walked, Phoebe dragged her hand with the stack of beaded bracelets along the white hallway wall. Izzy almost told Phoebe to stop. Izzy's mom was always reminding Izzy and Nate to be careful about leaving fingerprints on the walls. But she worried that Phoebe would just roll her eyes. And Izzy had no clue what she'd do then.

Thankfully, Phoebe raised her hand to flip her hair and gather it over her shoulder. The hair flip was a classic Daphne move. Izzy had tried to draw the motion on paper. The key to getting it right was in the head tilt and upturned eyes. But the faces Izzy drew always looked deep in thought, as if they were pondering the mysteries of the universe.

The opposite of what the expression looked like in real life.

They were almost to the bottom of the stairway when Phoebe stopped and pressed one finger to her lips. Izzy nodded. Phoebe's hunched shoulders and wide grin made Izzy feel like they were still little and wearing their jagged half-heart necklaces. Izzy was relieved that she hadn't said anything about fingerprints. This moment wouldn't have happened if she had.

Leaning with their backs against the stairway wall, they heard Phoebe's mom say, "I'm so sorry. That's really tough."

"We'll figure something out," said Izzy's mom. "I'm working on a few ideas."

"How's Greg handling it?" asked Phoebe's mom.

"You can imagine," said Izzy's mom.

Silence.

What would her mom figure out? What ideas was she

working on? Izzy leaned forward to peek around the corner. But Phoebe pressed Izzy back against the wall, as if they were about to hear something interesting and she didn't want Izzy to ruin the moment.

Greg was Izzy's dad. He fixed whatever was broken in their house—rattling pipes, flickering lights, loose-hinged doors that scraped the hardwood floors. Izzy's house was super old and her parents had spent years fixing it up. They'd torn down walls, ripped up tile, and peeled off wallpaper. Izzy's mom once spent an entire week polishing the doorknobs and window locks to restore their original color. So maybe that's what her mom was talking about?

But as the silence in the kitchen continued, Izzy began to worry that her mom was talking about something way more serious than home repairs.

Suddenly Phoebe jumped from the stairway to the kitchen floor. She landed with a thump.

"Phoebe," said Phoebe's mom. "You scared me."

"What were you guys talking about?" asked Phoebe.

"Nothing," said Izzy's mom. She stood up from

her stool and pressed her fingers against the corner of her eyes. *Was she about to cry?*

"Mom," said Izzy. "What's wrong?"

"Um, I think I might be getting a cold. It's terrible timing." Izzy's mom reached for a tissue. But instead of blowing her nose, she crumpled the tissue in her hand.

Izzy's mom was starting an interior-design business. Her first potential client was coming over that afternoon to see their house and get a sense of her mom's style. All afternoon she'd been plumping pillows, refolding blankets, and straightening picture frames. Even then, she stuffed the tissue in her pocket and looked around the kitchen like she was searching for a spill to wipe clean.

Phoebe picked a red grape from the ceramic bowl in the center of the island. She peeled off the skin before popping the grape in her mouth.

"Are you girls hungry?" asked Izzy's mom as she scrubbed an invisible spot the counter. "I have some frozen cookie dough in the freezer. I was going to put it in the oven later to give the house a homey smell, but I can do it now."

"Good idea," said Phoebe's mom. "What do you say, Phoebe? Want to stay for some cookies?"

Phoebe reached for another grape. "No, thanks. I'll eat at my sleepover."

"Oh," said Izzy's mom. "Okay." She glanced at Phoebe's mom.

Phoebe's mom shrugged, but just barely. As if maybe Izzy wouldn't notice.

Izzy hated how clueless they thought she was. About the cookie bribe. The shrug. The sleepover at Daphne's house that Izzy already knew about because she'd heard girls talking about it at school. The fact that Phoebe was suddenly not hungry even though she said she was starving a few minutes ago and kept reaching for grapes.

Izzy knew their moms wished that she and Phoebe were still babies so they could plop them down on a soft blanket with some squeaking toys and continue talking. But life wasn't that simple anymore. Phoebe had places to go. And Izzy was not invited.